Scent of the River

The story of Tsali and the Cherokee Removal

A novel

Frederick E. Bryson

Printed in Victoria, Canada

Note for Librarians: a cataloguing record for this book that includes Dewey Classification and US Library of Congress numbers is available from the National Library of Canada. The complete cataloguing record can be obtained from the National Library's online database at: www.nlc-bnc.ca/amicus/index-e.html

ISBN 1-4120-1560-X

This book was published on-demand in cooperation with Trafford Publishing. On-demand publishing is a unique process and service of making a book available for retail sale to the public taking advantage of on-demand manufacturing and Internet marketing. On-demand publishingincludes promotions, retail sales, manufacturing, order fulfilment, accounting and collecting royalties on behalf of the author.

Suite 6E, 2333 Government St., Victoria, B.C. V8T 4P4, CANADA
Phone 250-383-6864 Toll-free 1-888-232-4444 (Canada & US)
Fax 250-383-6804 E-mail sales@trafford.com
Web site www.trafford.com TRAFFORD PUBLISHING IS A DIVISION OF TRAFFORD HOLDINGS LTD.
Trafford Catalogue #03-1937 www.trafford.com/robots/03-1937.html

10 9 8 7 6 5 4

Dedication

This book is dedicated to John Wikle who, in an almost literal sense, put this pen in my hand; and to Jim Biggs to whom I owe a great debt of laughter.

Acknowledgements

My thanks to those who read the manuscript in-process, and provided guidance and suggestions, including Ray Gibson and Terri Krivich. Particular thanks go to a certain redhead who prodded me with ideas to sharpen the story and put it in historical context.

Cover

Art and argument for the cover was provided by Ann Bryson Martin of Vernon Hill, VA.

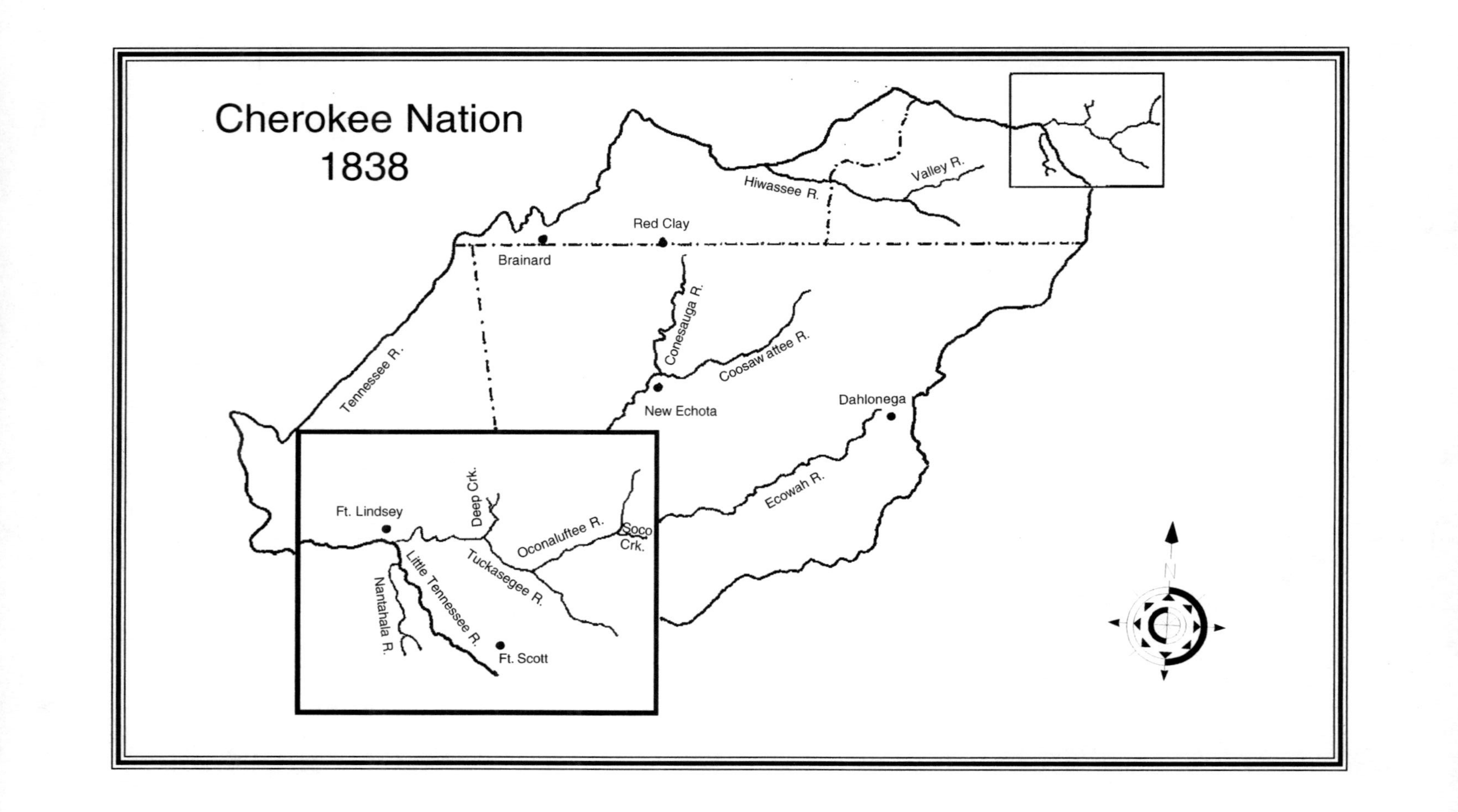
Cherokee Nation
1838
Hiwassee R.
Valley R.
Red Clay
Brainard
Conesauga R.
Coosaw attee R.
Tennessee R.
New Echota
Dahlonega
Ecowah R.
Ft. Lindsey
Deep Crk.
Oconaluftee R.
Soco
Crk.
Tuckasegee R.
Little Tennessee R.
Nantahala R.
Ft. Scott
N

Preface

In the years before Hernando Desoto, a loose confederation of intermarried aboriginal clans roamed the mountains and foothills of Southern Appalachia. They subsisted on agricultural staples of corn, beans, and squash, augmented by what they could catch or kill. Until the 1700 Century, most lived communally. The name they gave to themselves was the "Principal People," but because their language was derived from Iroquois, neighboring tribes referred to them as "chelokee," meaning people of a different speech. With the coming of White settlers that eventually surrounded their region, the name evolved to "Cherokee."

It was with these White neighbors that the Cherokees—as they had existed for some 10,000 years—met their final conflict.

From the perspective of over a century and a half, this story confirms what we are reluctant to admit: That government of law is often abrogated by the interest of self. The example involving the Cherokees was acted out in 1838 in what was known at the time as the Cherokee Nation. This was a political and geographic entity promulgated by tribal leaders who were clever enough to attempt a show of assimilation to White culture and wrap their own interests in the garment of democracy. In their struggle, they were pitted against the states of Georgia and Tennessee—and, unfortunately against the will of Andrew Jackson. During the period before and during Jackson's presidency, from 1829 through 1836, every chance was afforded the forces of reasonableness to prevail. The Cherokees drafted their own constitution, and declared themselves a virtual nation within a nation. Tests in the U.S. Supreme Court upheld their right to remain on their land, the land where they had lived for eons. Trade and exchange with White neighbors was conducted, for the most part, in peaceful terms, beneficial to both parties. Some Cherokees even embraced the White man's religion.

In spite of this, almost all of the Cherokees were forced by an army of 7,000 soldiers to emigrate to a resettlement tract in Oklahoma. Reparations of slightly more than $5 million were to be paid to compensate them for the loss of their homelands. Of the 16,000 people who began the journey west, about one-fourth died along the way.

The impetus to move the Cherokees was many sided. The prevailing mood of expansive growth in the U.S. at the time demanded more room for White settlers. For this reason, presidents as early as Thomas Jefferson suggested that the Indian tribes of the Southeast would be better off in the west, out of the way of expansion. This was highlighted in 1802 by an agreement between the federal government and the State of Georgia, allowing Georgia's claim to five counties in the northwest corner of the state that lay within the Cherokee Nation. The urgency within Georgia to secure these lands increased dramatically when gold was discovered there in 1829.

However, the powder in the flashpan of removal was Andrew Jackson. Jackson's enmity toward the leadership of the Cherokee Nation was hot and intractable. What is surprising is that twenty-five years before, these men had been allies. The Cherokees secured Jackson's reputation as a military tactician and, possibly, saved his life at the Battle of Horseshoe Bend, against the Creek Indians. But friendship turned to wrath when Jackson claimed 1.9 million acres in Alabama of former Creek land as payment for his military service. The Cherokee leadership, headed by Principal Chief John Ross, counter claimed, and won, earning Jackson's everlasting resentment. Even after Jackson left office and the Cherokees were in the middle of removal, Jackson continued to excoriate the Cherokee leadership.

Today, one man stands as an icon of resistance to the removal. Out of the thousands of people evicted, he and his family were the only ones to resist by force. This man was an aboriginal Cherokee who farmed a 14-acre tract of land in the high mountain region of North Carolina. In a census of the time, he is described as ". . . living in the fourth house on the Nantahala River ," presumably upstream from the confluence with the Little Tennessee into which it flows. His name was Tsali, or, in the anglicized version, Charley.

In more than a century and a half after his death, the character of Tsali has been embellished such that he has come to be viewed as a combination of Robin Hood and Joan of Arc, sacrificing himself so that the remainder of his people could stay in their homelands. In reality, he was neither. At the time of removal, he was the patriarch of a modest family, a 60-year old hunter/gatherer, like his neighbors. If he spoke English at all, it would have been minimal.

He and his family had avoided the early roundups of Cherokees that had begun under General Winfield Scott in May of 1838. They were among thc last to be captured, on the last day of October of that year.

What happened on November 1 is the source of his legend. As Tsali's family was being marched down the Tuckasegee River, escorted by four regular army soldiers, they rebelled, killing two of the soldiers and gravely wounding a third. Only the officer in charge—a Lieutenant A. J. Smith—escaped unharmed.

This is the story of how the wills of two men—one president, one native farmer, neither of which knew the other—came into conflict and how the conflict was concluded.

Deep Creek
Cherokee Nation
November 24, 1838

Just before dawn, Tsali crawled from beneath the low rock overhang where he had slept, to the edge of a long drop. He looked down into the steep valley of the stream that, as it ran downhill and grew larger, would become known as Deep Creek. High up on the mountain, the November air was cold and wet and he pulled a blanket around him and sat cross-legged on a boulder. His old body no longer lived this life well. Joints ached in the damp air and his back grew stiff from sleeping on the ground. He missed his cabin on the far Nantahala. Later in the day, maybe it would be warmer and the hunting would be good, should he decide to stay. If he did, he would eat rabbit tonight, or squirrel. Perhaps he could even chance a fire near the mouth of the shallow cave where he slept. A squirrel would be good. A rabbit would be even better, easier to chew. It had been a long time since he had eaten meat or slept in something soft. Up here, the cold would never go away and a fire was risky, so he had laid in the low shelter beneath the rock in a space that would barely hold a groundhog, thinking about his wife, about his sons and daughter, about his grandchildren, and about his home on their high farmlands. Sleep came sometimes.

It had been raining now for days and a mist rose and swirled in the air above the valley where it mixed with the faint smell of a distant campfire. He had come to this place that was far from his home after the killing, because it was the one place where he knew that the men in uniforms could not go. It was a place made for bears and foxes, tangled and dense. All around the spot where he sat, a laurel thicket covered the flanks of the mountain like a collar. No man with a horse or boots or sword or rifle would come here. Only an Indian who did not want to be found would come here—or another Indian looking for one who did not want to be found.

Behind him, a crow announced his presence to inhabitants on the ridge. Inwardly, Tsali smiled. The crow was wise, as were the mist and the mountain, for they knew the secret of everlastingness. Tsali made a wish for this wisdom, then waited with his mind receptive for it to come to him, as he had been taught many years ago by his grandfather. When it did not come, he waited some more. A cold wind came up and washed over his lined brown face and hair that had gone mostly gray, but he made no movement to protect himself because, perhaps, in the wind there was wisdom. But there was not, at least, not for him, not today. The wind was only cold, and it made his sixty-year-old knees ache more. The only wisdom that he sensed was to realize that the noisy crow could not tell him the secret of everlastingness because it only had to eat and nest and tell the other creatures of the mountain about the comings and goings of strangers. It had nothing to decide and did not know the secret of making decisions. Neither did the mist nor the mountain. They only had to be. They knew nothing of the awful curse of Spear-Finger that he had brought on himself.

Perhaps because he had been alone on the mountain for the better part of a month, his attention drifted and Tsali thought of his father and wondered what he would decide if he were in Tsali's predicament. When Tsali was a boy, his father had seemed to have wisdom. He had taught the boy the simple things, to be respectful of the animals that they killed and to ask their understanding for taking their lives. Looking out over the descending mountains, he puzzled over why he could not have his father's wisdom now instead of his father's axe. The axe had been a good gift; indeed, he used it almost every day, to kill the small animals that they cooked or to trim the bark off a limb or to cut wood for the fire. But the axe was of no use to him in this matter that he had to decide now. It still had blood on it where it had struck a soldier in the forehead. Now he needed wisdom more than he needed the axe.

He thought of his wife, Nancy, too. Had it been her frailness and exhaustion that had pushed them to attack the soldiers? The soldiers had been impatient and had tried to make them march faster, but in their self-important haste he could not say that they had been unkind. The officer had even put her on his own horse where she and one of the younger children could ride. Still, the forced march had been enough to enrage Tsali, along with everything else that had happened with the removal of his people to the west. The soldiers. The prodding of them like cattle. The taking of their homes in the mountains where they had lived since before the telling of legends. The arrival of the White settlers on the heels of the soldiers, to scavenge their possessions. Something happened among the Indians as Tsali's little party was being moved. Something happened all at once. There was a look that passed between them, Tsali and his son-in-law, Chutequutlutlih, then Chutequutlutlih buried the axe in the head of a soldier. The others attacked the remaining soldiers, killing one and wounding a third. One—the lieutenant—escaped on a free horse, perhaps his own. For this, the soldiers stalked Tsali as he would stalk a rabbit. Out there, far down below the mist, men were waiting for him to come out.

None of this would have happened, except for the will of one man who had lived in a place they called Washington, a man whose life had been saved years before from Creek warriors by Tsali's friend Junaluska. They say that they gave the man the name of a tree, Old Hickory, in an act of respect. Junaluska was gone now, along with the others, to the west. Even Old Hickory was gone from Washington now. But others had come to carry on his will, and the soldiers were still out there somewhere, waiting for him, waiting for Tsali to come out of the thicket where they could not get him. They would wait, he knew, perhaps forever.

Late yesterday, just before the sun had set, his friend Euchella of the Oconaluftee Band came from a long walk down on the Little Tennessee River and brought him news about his wife and also told him the other news, about his older sons and the husband of his daughter. After they shared the familiar greeting of grasping each other's arms, Euchella told his story, told it the way a Cherokee would tell it, plain, the way that Tsali had told Euchella earlier in the year about the death of his wife: "They were tried and executed at the mouth of the Tuckasegee. Wachacha and the rest of us did it. I, myself, shot Chutequutlutlih. Wasseton was spared by Col. Foster because he is only sixteen." He had said all this in a heavy voice, but with a hand near his knife.

Tsali knew Euchella to be an angry man. He had reason. A generation younger than Tsali, he, too, had resisted removal, and had hidden out in the mountains of the high Snowbirds. He hated this removal as much as Tsali did because his own wife and young daughter had starved while he hid. His face was dark with all this trouble as he conveyed the news. But at the moment, he hated Tsali, too, for the compromise in which he found himself. Euchella had walked up the trail by Deep Creek. He had known where to look for Tsali. Ten or eleven days before, soldiers had come into the valley looking for him; a good scout would have found signs. But the soldiers could not get their horses through the laurel thickets and up the steep slopes that were slick from the rain, so they turned back as Tsali had counted on them doing. Today, Euchella had come back on foot with others from the Oconaluftee Band, then moved up-stream by himself from the camp, to sit and wait to see if Tsali would appear. Tsali had watched him from the edge of the rock, then went down to meet him, far below the spot where he had been hiding.

Euchella had grown into a brutal man. A head taller than Tsali, his face was lean and hinted of rage that would not be quiet and frustration that cannot be ignored. Perhaps, that is why he delivered his news with such brutality. Or, perhaps, it was because Tsali had brought him bad news in the early part of the year. As the man spoke, Tsali tried to show no emotion, but there was a tightening in his mouth. Canantutlaga, his eldest, dead. Lau in nih, his second born, dead. Chutequutlutlih, the husband of his daughter, Ancih, dead. But Wasseton lived. Wasseton, the son of Lau in nih, lived.

So now Tsali knew how serious the soldiers were. From the moment his son-in-law had swung his axe at the head of the soldier named Perry and grabbed his gun, he knew that something like this would be the outcome. He had acted and the others had acted with him, and in that minute two soldiers were dead on the ground. The officer who led them fled to find more soldiers who were at that time only about a half mile away. When the soldiers returned, the Indians began to run, back up the river towards the mountains. They argued along the way about where to go. Nancy could not travel far. Neither could she stay in the mountains as Tsali wished. She would die there. Reluctantly, Tsali agreed to let her double back with their sons, to their home on the high Nantahala. He would lead the soldiers away, but he did not like their parting. He could no longer protect her. His only comfort was that he did not believe that the soldiers wanted her. He thought that they would come for him and his sons. "The soldiers will see this as murder," he had insisted. "To them, this is not war to protect our homes and our lands. We must hide or die." But the younger men said that, no, they would not hide. They would fight them again if the soldiers came back. Anyhow, they said that they were too clever to be caught again by soldiers. But it had not been the soldiers who came back, it had been Euchella and his band. And now his sons and his son-in-law were dead, shot yesterday.

This was not the end of Euchella's bad news. He explained to Tsali that not only were the soldiers searching all the coves and cabins for him, but that what he had done in killing those two brought trouble and shame to his people. Among the Cherokees, he was not being talked as a warrior and a man of honor, but as an outcast, one who had made their misery worse. Tsali was stunned. It was the soldiers who were robbing him and his tribe of their homes and their farms, it was the soldiers who were rounding up the people with no notice and forcing them into stockades where many had died of the heat in the summer. It was the soldiers who were putting the people on the boats and wagon trains and sending them off to a far place called Oklahoma, with nothing except what they wore. Yet, here was this man, the friend who was the son of a friend, telling him that he was cursed by his people for resisting and fighting the soldiers. "They say that you must be marked for death like Spear-Finger because you have brought calamity on the people of the Oconaluftee. It is nothing that can be forgiven at the time of the Corn Festival."

Spear-Finger. He said Spear-Finger, that she-bitch murderess from the ageless legends of the Cherokees, who had been burned, burned so that the Principal People could be cleansed of her crime. The people said Tsali was like Spear-Finger. He sat down heavily.

Euchella had one more thing to explain. "I've told you that we executed your sons. This is true. But it was part of a pact my people made with Col. Foster who is now in charge of the soldiers. He was sent here by the big general, the one they call Scott, to find you, to try you, and to punish you. But he has made this arrangement with us that if you are brought in that the rest of our people who remain here who are not already citizens can stay."

"Why did he do this?"

"Because the soldiers want you badly. They say their national honor must be avenged, and if you stay here, they cannot get you."

"They want me that much?"

Euchella nodded. "That much."

"What will happen to me if I come in?"

"We will shoot you."

"What if I am innocent?"

Euchella took a breath. "There is no innocence.

You have already been found guilty. You cannot be found innocent. You provide too much justification for this removal and the years of robbing us of our land. You represent the 'beast' the White people want removed from this country," he said shaking his fist in the air. Then he bent toward Tsali and continued in a whisper. "They have tried you because it is their law, the same as ours. A death must be avenged. But they want you dead because you have mocked them for nearly a month and they cannot stand it. They are not a patient people. It is an embarrassment for them that you are alive."

Tsali was silent for a long time; his age seemed to descend on him all at once. Then he asked the question that he did not want to ask: "If the soldiers cannot find me, why did they send you, Euchella? We have hunted together, since you were a boy. You have eaten at my fire as much as at your fathers. Why did they send you?"

Euchella scowled as if he were cornered and his anger resurfaced. "Because Euchella must be the instrument to destroy you because you have become like Spear-Finger. I must 'cleanse' the Cherokees of a murderer who has brought a wrath upon us. You know the Blood Law as well as I know it. Harmony must be restored."

Tsali felt the weight of his stigma. His wife would be shunned, the memory of his sons dishonored. He was glad that his father could not see this. Well, there was nothing that he could do about that now.

He would go back up the mountain and think about what to do. He told Euchella that he would give him an answer in a day or two. He would either go with them to the fort where the soldiers were and be shot there, or fight them and die here as a Cherokee, on the mountain where Deep Creek begins.

Dahlonega
Georgia
May, 1831

The three old friends stood on a hillside north of the settlement of Dahlonega and watched the commotion below. They would have liked to go closer, but did not dare because the White settlers there might have attacked them. Gold had been discovered there two years before, and the settlers were extremely protective of their claims. Sometimes, it was said, they even shot each other over disputes. Soldiers milled about their bivouac in a field outside the village, while mounted officers shouted orders as their horses wheeled. Sergeants echoed the orders and somehow brought order. On the dirt road that ran like an ochre strip—north to south—through the cluster of buildings, the blue uniforms began to form lines as the sound of a drummer tapping cadence filled the valley. Civilians watching from plank sidewalks were in a festive mood and waved as the assembled soldiers stood impassively, awaiting orders to march.

Standing on the hill in the warm spring sun, John Ross took in the developments with satisfaction. Although only fractionally Indian, Ross was the Principal Chief of the Cherokee Nation, numbering some twenty-two thousand souls scattered over a great oval of Appalachia that lay in parts of five states. He had been chief for four years, a task to which he felt born. Unlike his other two friends who stood with him, Ross felt no ambivalence about what he saw. The federals were leaving his land, the land which the small part of him that was Indian loved reverently. Now, the Cherokees would have a chance to settle the almost thirty-year dispute that his nation had with the White State of Georgia, without interference from an army of White soldiers.

It was also the army of his nemesis, Andrew Jackson. Practical man that he fancied himself to be, Ross did not like to even think of Jackson because what came to mind was always irrational. The very mention of Jackson caused bitterness to settle over him. There was something elementary in Jackson's nature that had always annoyed Ross, ever since he had served under him at Horseshoe Bend, back in '13. It surprised Ross that people could not see Jackson for what he was. The United States had elected a "man of the people," or so they thought. Ross knew better. Jackson was anything but that. Jackson was a self-aggrandizing, White supremacist thief. There, he said it, if only to himself. It had taken him almost twenty years to form those words. But at least now the soldiers of Jackson were leaving the Cherokee Nation.

The other two men standing on the hill with him would not entirely agree with his relief, Ross realized. One of them, Kahnungdatlageh, who now preferred to be called by his White name, Major Ridge, did not believe that the departure of the troops was a good thing. Ridge was his oldest friend in the Cherokee Nation—and the most eloquent. When words were needed in council meetings, Ridge was never lacking and was always supportive. Still, this thing about the soldiers separated them. Ridge was prosperous—rich, even—his farm and orchards near New Echota were enormous. To him, the soldiers represented stability at a time when the Georgians were becoming more unpredictable and aggressive. In a dark moment, Ridge had mumbled that the Cherokees might not be able to hold out against the Georgians if the soldiers were not around to keep peace. But Ridge spoke the words of a defensive old man who had, perhaps, too much to protect. Maybe it was true what was said that the "spring had gone out of his bow." Ross suspected that, had Ridge been chosen chief four years earlier, the Cherokees would now be loading wagons to passively move west as the president and the Georgians wanted. But Ross was not Ridge, and he felt his feet involuntarily digging into the soil of the hill.

The third member of their party was harder to read. Chief of the Snowbird Clan that lived high in the mountains in North Carolina, Junaluska seemed untouched by the turmoil that swirled around much of the rest of the Cherokee Nation. But Junaluska was, Ross believed, their history, not their future. He was from an Over Hill clan, whereas Ridge and Ross were of Lower Town clans. It was men like himself and Ridge's son John who were what the Cherokees would become, educated, Christian, democratic. Junaluska's clan lived almost exactly as the Cherokees lived 500 years before. Ross had seen their village along Tullula Creek, and they still kept a communal corn crib into which the clan stored grain against the winter. Beside each cabin was a small sleeping hut that was easy to warm. Boys were still taught to hunt with the bow, should their supply of black powder run out. They trapped and skinned animals and often wore those skins, as Junaluska unselfconsciously did now. Junaluska was a primitive, what they called a "full blood." But he was wise and pure of heart, and probably respected more than any other member of the tribe. That is why Ross asked him to join them in Dahlonega. He needed to know how Junaluska felt.

Politician that he was—and he disliked the word—Ross was aware that men like Junaluska were still the majority of the Principal People. They survived on what they could grow in small gardens and by hunting. Their diet was plenty, without being abundant, and, unlike their Lower Town kin, they tended to be lean. It was a private joke with Ross that he could tell the altitude at which a Cherokee lived by the leanness of his body. Such was the case with Ross and his two companions. Both he and Ridge were what could be kindly described as corpulent, their prosperity visible around their waists. Junaluska, on the other hand, was still lean, although stooped a bit now with age.

The thing that politician Ross needed to know from Junaluska was how much he and others like him were willing to resist the Removal Act that Andrew Jackson had squeezed through the U.S. Congress. Would Junaluska be like Ridge, reluctant but willing to move, or would he resist up to the point of declaring war?

For a moment, the attention of the three was drawn to the scene below as the first of the soldiers began to move out.

"Why do you take so much pleasure in their departure?" Ridge asked in his voice that seemed to come from a deep cavern.

"Because I grew up Cherokee," was all the Principal Chief replied.

"What will you now do to keep order? Look at those people down there. The soldiers are the only thing that keeps them from rising against us. Nothing—not even their own law—will keep them from the gold that lies in these hills," he said, pointing far to their left, to a cut in a hillside where men had made enormous digs. "I have seen them. Gold makes them crazier than whiskey."

"We have our own law," Ross said, shuffling his feet. In truth, he did not know what he would do if the settlers attacked. If it were a mass, coordinated attack, he assumed that his people would gather in kind and counterattack. What he feared most was a protracted struggle of attrition where the Georgians would raid in small parties and, like horseflies, bite them unexpectedly. But Ross was not a war chief and he did not have the cunning necessary for it. As a child, his weapon of choice had been the pen. That weapon had served him well. He had not killed men in battle as had Ridge and Junaluska. Indeed, he had been a scribe with Jackson's forces at Horseshoe Bend, embellishing the deeds of the leader whom he later came to loathe. Perhaps it was his loathing of Andrew Jackson that now filled him with such joy to see the representatives of the man leaving. Could it be that his relief blinded him to the reality to come? "We have our police, our courts," he offered finally.

Ridge was quick to jump on the weakness of this. "The Cherokee police can act only after a crime has been committed. What can we—the Chickamaugah here in Georgia—do to keep the settlers from raiding us?"

"We will find a way," Ross replied stubbornly, sounding more passive than he wished.

"We are still Cherokee," Junaluska spoke for the first time.

The other two knew what that meant. As a people, they lived by a code that was based on retribution. What was done to them as a crime must be avenged. It was their law, the Blood Law.

Ross knew, however, that it was a law that they, as a nation, might not be able to maintain. There was something akin to a New Testament/Old Testament split in his people, with those of the Lower Towns following a path of assimilation and negotiation with the encroaching White world. The Over Hill clans in the mountains had no need of negotiation because there were almost no Whites there, aside from a few traders such as the man Will Thomas who lived with the Oconaluftee clan. These Cherokees continued to live by the old rules, to celebrate the Corn Festival, to revere their dreams, and to seek counsel from the Great Spirit. To them, commerce meant trading skins for a knife, and Black slaves, as both he and Ridge kept to work their farms, would be nothing but an absurd burden to men like Junaluska. As for the soldiers, it was clear that to Junaluska they could stay or leave, it made no difference. He and his people would go on as before.

For a moment, Ross felt overwhelmed. Could he hold them all together as a nation, or would they split along the fissure represented by his two friends here?

As the troops left the little town below and marched south toward the railway center in the distant village of Atlanta, the three Indians heard a whoop come up from the crowd below. Each knew what that meant, that the settlers were now being set free to do what they wanted. And what they wanted were the five counties in North Georgia that lay within the boundary of the Cherokee Nation. How these three could keep them from getting their hands on this land was something that they were going to have to figure out.

Washington
District of Columbia
June, 1832

Andrew Jackson was filled with anger and secrets. He'd been angry for as long as he could remember. Being president had not alleviated the fury that lurked in his mind like a nocturnal predator, the fury that he worked hard to keep hidden. He sometimes wondered why he tried. Everyone with whom he came in contact suspected it—from congressmen to servants—sooner or later. Only a few did not fear it. All through his political and military life, the newspapers had been rife with rumors of his fights and duels and horse whippings. And sure enough, he bore scars to support the stories, including several that were not publicly known. "Old Hickory" they called him, initially because he marched his troops with unbending discipline, but later because when he became enraged and struck an opponent, the person felt as though he'd been battered by an unbending hickory stick.

Now, in old age, that kind of violent trouble was well behind him, relegated to the days when he carried his hickory cane because it became a personal trademark. Today, he needed the damned thing just to get around. And sometimes it became a handy instrument of his temper, as it was now when he reacted to the unrelenting throb in his left shoulder. Moving slowly through his bedroom in the White House, he struck the cane against a bedpost with a report that rung around the room. His butler, almost used to these sharp sounds emanating from the president's room, poked his head through the doorway. Seeing fire in the old man's face, he quickly jerked his head back out and resumed his stiff stance outside the door.

Only Andy Jackson knew the whole truth about his temper. His wife, Rachel, had known when she was alive, but now that she was gone, no one else understood it and his struggle to keep it in balance. Perhaps, that was why her death left such a hole in his life. She had known that his temper served as a mask that hid an altogether different sort of man who could, at times, be more boy than man. Rachel had understood that Andrew was a poser, a youth who had been thrust into manhood by an earlier war, a British saber, and his mother's sudden and ugly death from cholera. Over the years, his temper had come to be as much a part of him as the blue of his eyes or his gray shock of hair that often looked as if it did not know which way to go. Being president had not helped. In the three and a half years that he had been in office, he had discovered there were many things, great and small, that the power of the presidency could not change.

Jackson knew that if his temper had nearly killed him—as it had on at least three occasions—then it had also saved him. It showed itself in two ways: One was a hot, passionate, consuming fury; the other was an icy, quiet hatred. As a boy, when he had been a prisoner of the British, an officer struck him in the left hand and face with his saber. Indignant at being told to polish the officer's boots, the boy hotly refused. But after he was wounded, the cold fury took over and held him together. Bleeding and in extreme pain, he did not cry out, but, rather, a rigid, sustaining hatred came over him. This was the first episode of what was to become a pattern, wild outrage followed by cold determination.

A pattern. He believed in patterns. Men were defined by patterns. Even Andrew Jackson, President of the United States. Sitting down on the edge of the bed, he pulled his robe about him and tilted his head back. He thought of Rachel. He thought of New Orleans. He thought of the campaign in Florida, and the election of '24, the one that had been stolen from him by Adams. But these were not the things that defined him. What defined him was Charles Dickinson.

As a young man, he and Charles Dickinson of Nashville—a man known to be the best duelist in Tennessee—quarreled bitterly. It did not start that way, but Rachel's name came up, about them not being legally married the first time they were married. Then Dickinson wrote a letter, calling him a "coward and an equivocator," Jackson exploded with red rage and challenged Dickinson to a duel. But it was the cold, settling hatred that took over during the duel, just as it had after the British soldier struck him. He remembered it even now, over twenty-five years later.

As they lined up eight paces apart, he felt the familiar icy calm. He would let Dickinson shoot first. Better to be dead than to be at this man's mercy.

Dickinson was a good shot, but not perfect. There was a loud report and a puff of dust from the front of Jackson's coat. The bullet lodged against his ribs, maybe an inch from his heart. The pain almost drove him to his knees; it was as though a gandy dancer had driven a rail spike into his chest. Clenching his teeth, he took a careful breath through his nose. It hurt like all hell. Covering the spot with his left hand, he could smell the smoke and sense the silence of the others. He would stand. The calm held, and kept the pain at bay a little.

Astonished, Dickinson retreated. Jackson's

second, John Overton, raised his pistol at Dickinson, as custom dictated. "Back to the mark, sir!" cried Overton. Dickinson returned to his position. Jackson raised his pistol, took aim, and squeezed the trigger. The hammer stopped at the half-cocked position. Again, he reset the hammer and squeezed. This time it fired, hitting Dickinson just below the rib cage. The man wilted to the ground. Moments later, after the attending surgeon had examined the dying Dickinson, he came over to Jackson and noted that there was blood puddling on his shoe. As the doctor examined him and found that he had at least one rib broken, Jackson's only remark was that he would have shot Dickinson even if he had been shot through the brain. That was part of his pattern.

Over the years, Dickinson's bullet remained as a lump between his ribs, a reminder of the hidden balancing act that he performed. The ball still pained him when he twisted his body, like a sharp voice of conscience that only he could hear. He hoped that voice would keep him in check through today. This morning, his mood was especially black. Those damned Cherokees from Georgia and North Carolina and his home state of Tennessee had the temerity to insist on seeing him about this removal issue. He grunted. After how they had helped him fight the Creeks in Georgia and later at Horseshoe Bend, it would be political suicide to refuse them. He would appear to be an ingrate.

As he rose from the bed, he was remembering again. This time he remembered the days of almost twenty years ago and the men the Cherokee Nation had sent to him for the campaign against the Red Stick Creeks. His eyes narrowed. Ridge was there; Jackson was the one to give him the rank of major.

But it was John Ross whom he remembered most. Ross had helped him with the war against the Creeks, but had gotten in the way ever since . . . in the way by making a stink when his Tennessee boys, including, Davy Crockett, had helped themselves to the livestock of the Cherokees on their way home from Horseshoe Bend . . . in the way when the Indians had slipped into Washington and absolutely stole the land on the south side of the Tennessee River that he had set aside for himself and his friends as war reparations from the Creeks . . . in the way, generally, by bollixing up the movement of White settlers westward.

What angered him most was that the Cherokees might have him in a box. Horseshoe Bend was a box that held a lot of secrets, most of which Jackson preferred to keep secret. It was the battle on which he had founded his reputation as a military strategist. But it had not been Jackson's tactics that won the battle. Jackson had ordered a cannon barrage on the Creek encampment, from across the river. But the Creeks had dug in, and all that the cannon shot struck was empty earth. After two hours of bombardment, not a single Creek was killed. When the barrage stopped, they emerged, ready to fight.

What turned the battle was when Major Ridge led a band of his North Georgia Cherokees across the river and set loose the Creek canoes. Agitated, the Creeks came out of their holes to attack. Jackson's forces then caught them in a crossfire and cut them down. Before they fled, more than half were dead. There was much skinning that night. Many belts were made from the skin of Creek warriors. It was good for Jackson that this secret did not get out.

And there was one more. One of the Cherokees had saved Jackson's life at Horseshoe Bend. Jackson had never publicly acknowledged the fact that in the afternoon of the pivotal charge, old chief Junaluska had pulled a Creek warrior off him, just as the Indian was about to bury his club in Jackson's head. Jackson was weak, still recovering from another dueling wound, one that had nearly required his left arm to be amputated. But he had hidden the truth of this incident all these years. Not even Rachel had known. Now, his humiliation at having been saved by a Cherokee lay like another bullet in his ribs. If they could prove it . . . if. He needed to know what they were prepared to say.

Jackson moved to a chair that had an embroidered seat, and arms that ended with ornate carved heads of lionesses. It was his favorite chair in the bedroom. He loved the presidency. Lord, God, he wished that his mother could see all this. His last memory of her was as she attended the wounded soldiers in the infirmary in Charleston. And Rachel. She had lived with him for so long, only to miss all this splendor. How much better it would have been if she could have been with him. She had known how he felt about the Cherokees, but not why . She had known almost nothing about John Ross, except that he had been a troublesome Indian Chief, and, oddly, almost a White man at that.

Jackson struck the wall with his cane. After he was elected president, Ross refused—refused! —to meet with him at the Hermitage after the Removal Bill passed. What gall! Why the hell didn't they just go and do what both Jefferson and Madison had suggested long before, move to the west and get the hell out of the way?

But Cherokees were stubborn creatures, and tricky, too. When you bribed them, they didn't stay bribed. They wanted more. In spite of their help, or maybe because of it, Jackson did not like them. They were too clever and they knew it. The Cherokees had adapted to the White man's ways and had even used these ways to solidify their own position. Cherokee Nation, indeed. There was no such thing as a Cherokee Nation! They had gone to the trouble to make up their own alphabet and write a constitution to support this bogus claim to nationhood. Hell and pitch. They couldn't even spell constitution before the White man came along.

He flicked his cane against the leg of a dresser. It made a loud, satisfying crack that caused his butler to jump again. This morning, he would have the last word on them, maybe. This morning, the tables would finally be turned, maybe. There was no more Madison to whom they could appeal. And Chief Justice Marshall, with all his opinions, could not help them. Marshall had no troops, and no court justice of the young republic had ever commanded an army. In an odd way, Jackson had waited all his adult life for this moment. John Ross. Yes, John Ross. Although John Ross would not be present—nay, would not be allowed— at the meeting to come, it would be Jackson's moment to horsewhip Ross. He had waited for this, even if he had to do it indirectly.

Jackson bellowed for his clothes. "Let's engage the enemy!" he shouted through the White House.

Soco Creek
Cherokee Nation
August, 1832

Jonas Jenkins always knew that he was different. It was like a birthright. For one thing, he had a life-long premonition that he would live so long that by the time he died, he would have outlived family and friends and be surrounded by faces that he only vaguely knew. This sense of certainty came to him as a small boy. Born in the then new state of Tennessee, in a new century, and in a new country, he seemed predestined to live a life that would be punctuated by history. That was fine with him, he supposed.

It was the other part of the birthright that troubled him some. He was a temperate man, a quiet man, and to the limit of his comprehension, a reflective man. To others, however, he seemed aloof and sometimes a little strange. Perhaps it was because he lived much of the time within himself, with memories and with an almost dreamy contemplation of things around him. In a later time, he would have been said to have an aura, a kind of untouchable quality that would allow him to, in the biblical phrase, walk harmlessly through the valley of the shadow of death. Not a maker of events, but an observer, Jonas sensed that his life would be like a scroll onto which the actions of his generation were recorded, the scroll of a country that was still gathering itself.

Perhaps it was the tug of history in the making that led him, at the age of eighteen, away from Tennessee, to the home state of Washington, Jefferson, Madison, and Monroe. And although he felt the journey was vaguely like a religious calling, he wished that his family had protested more when he left for the Shenandoah. He knew that they, too, thought him strange because they were often silent when he was present.

In Shenandoah City, he met and married Juliet Burkholder and the line of his own clan continued. Within a year, Jonas took his new wife to the difficult, but serenely beautiful mountains in North Carolina, not far from the ridge from which the state of his birth had been politically separated. In a steep valley called Soco Creek, in the shadow of the highest peaks of the Smokies, Jonas picked a southerly facing cove for his land, and laid a rock foundation for their cabin on a knoll. Within the foundation, he dug a root cellar so that Juliet would not have to venture outside to retrieve stored food. He laboriously squared the logs for the house so that they would fit tightly with little chinking. A chimney stood in the back of the house, along the north wall, and the opening of the fireplace was large enough to cook over and warm the cabin. On each side of the house ran a small stream, fed by springs that seeped from the sides of the cove. Jonas built a spring house out of stone over the smaller of the two. Milk for the spring house was supplied by a cow that he pastured on the westerly slope of the cove. He farmed a narrow flat strip that lay below his house, along Soco Creek.

Unlike Tennessee and Virginia, this was an untraveled place, as difficult to get a wagon through as it was to plow a straight furrow. Everywhere it was rocky and steep, and the mountainsides were covered with a dark shroud of balsam and spruce. The streams were too small and swift for navigation, and they flooded in an instant when rains came. As often as not, a thick fog covered the valley when he emerged from his cabin early in the morning. This was a moody, spiritual place, one to which Jonas could feel a connection that he did not fully understand. In Virginia, he had felt the energy and idealism of the new country; here, he felt a link to something much older.

At dawn before his wife stirred, Jonas often rose and sat on a rounded slab of gray granite that lay broken off from even larger pieces, beside Soco Creek. As the day grew brighter, he could smell the unique scent of the creek in the humid air, as it tore its way down the valley. The smell of it was different than the larger Oconaluftee into which it flowed, and also different than that of the Tuckasegee to the west, which absorbed the Oconaluftee. One scent was not more or less pleasant than another, just different; nor could one be accurately described, except to say that the Oconaluftee smelled colder, if such a thing could be said. Jonas was aware that he had never made this distinction in Tennessee or Virginia. Back then, a river had been just been a river. But here, had he been blindfolded and led to one after another, he could have identified each, in turn. Whatever instinct guided him to this land in the first place had also rewarded him with this heightened awareness. But he resolved not to tell anyone about it, even his wife, lest they think him stranger than they already did.

His bond with this land came early, formed with the help of the Indians who mostly peopled this place. Jonas had moved here because of the land. In Virginia, he had heard that the Cherokee Nation had relinquished its claim to this part of its holdings, opening it up for White settlers. When they arrived in 1821, Jonas and Juliet lived in their wagon until Jonas could fell enough trees to start their cabin.

Sometime during their first spring, their garden received a blessing in the form of a donation when a small Indian boy named Euchella appeared, bearing seeds for corn, beans, and squash. In a serious, almost reverent voice, he called them the "three sisters." He had traveled about a mile from his home, carrying seeds in a leather pouch. As he got to know the boy's family, Jonas learned from Euchella's mother that the Cherokees sustained themselves on these three plants, supplementing their diet with the occasional squirrel, rabbit, opossum, raccoon, and fish. As time passed, Jonas and Juliet were able to repay the kindness of their Indian neighbors with pieces of cloth or extra buttons or a small bag of corn meal. Jonas knew a little about farming, too, and suggested to Euchella that his mother not rely only on burying a fish with her spring seeds, that, instead of burning them, to take the stalks and leaves from the previous year's crop and bury them where she would plant the next year.

To Jonas, his Indian neighbors were respectful, even cautiously curious of Juliet and him. But there remained a great gulf between them. For all their similarity of circumstance, they could not have lived more differently. For instance, in matters of agriculture, Jonas noticed that it was always Euchella's mother and sisters who worked the field, planting, weeding, harvesting. Euchella's father and Euchella, himself, lived as much in the woods and along Soco Creek as they did in their home. The men would come and go without boundaries or schedule or direction. Even as a small boy, Euchella could be seen setting off on a trek as Jonas sat perched in morning meditation on his favorite rock by the stream. He believed that the boy knew that he was observed, but in these brief glimpses of each other, neither acknowledged the presence of the other. It was obvious that, to the boy, his journey, however short, was serious, private business. Had he wanted conversation, he would come to Jonas directly, calling out his approach to the household as was the Indian custom of courtesy. Otherwise, he did not expect a smile or a wave or a greeting, and preferred it that way.

Another thing that separated Indians from Whites was, of course, language. Indian speech sounded completely incomprehensible to Jonas. There were sounds within it that could not be formed in his throat. The Indians, on the other hand, mostly understood English, but were reluctant to use it except where politeness called for them to do so. They could accept benefits such as clothing and buttons and good steel knives, but the language seemed to be an artifact of European life for which they did not care. There was an aloofness about them when it came to language that bordered on superiority.

The thing that Jonas found most startling about these people, however, was their play. To him, more than anything else, this defined the difference between the two peoples. Games that White people played had, as their purpose, fun; the Cherokees played for pain. In White men's games, one played to win or for money. In Indian games, one played to survive. Throughout the year, whenever one village challenged another, or particularly during important festivals such as the Green Corn Festival, they played a game in which each player carried a stick. These sticks were about three and one-half feet long. On the end, was a netted cup, roughly five inches in diameter. Teams of players used these sticks to pass a leather ball that was half the size of a man's fist. The object was to carry the ball across goal lines at each end of the playing field. The sticks were marvelous for propelling the ball down the field. At the first game that he witnessed, Jonas stood and watched players pass to each other over distances of thirty or more yards. Strategy seemed to be that the team with the ball would protect the ball holder by blocking members of the other team from getting to him. Then, they would send one or more of their fastest runners down the field and the ball holder would fling the ball toward the runner. Ideally, the runner would either catch the ball in the air or scoop it up off the ground with his stick. Until he had it in the webbing of his stick, he could not touch the ball. Then, he would run across the goal line and toss the ball into the air. But between the point where he caught the ball and the goal line lay the difference between White games and Indian games. At this point, the sticks in the hands of opposing players became weapons and they could do anything with them to the ball carrier, if they could catch him. They could club, whack, gouge, and trip him. In a few cases, the ball carrier was known to put the ball in his mouth, but if caught, he would be choked with a stick until he spat it out.

At first, the savagery of the games horrified Jonas. Men were often maimed in what looked to be acts of barely controlled blood lust. But as the years passed, he came to understand the delicately balanced state of harmony in which the Cherokees lived. In domestic matters, they were mostly polite, respectful, unobtrusive. Women were accorded high standing and children were indulged. But to remain in balance, this tranquility required a counterweight. And for this, the stick-ball games served well.

White House
Washington, DC
April, 1833

ndrew Jackson heard the sound of a hard, persistent cough down the hall from his bedroom. It was Emily Donelson, the niece of his dead wife, who served as hostess in the White House. The cough had become an unwanted guest, showing up at inopportune moments. He was not good with sick people, and sought a distraction as he was fond of her and the cough gave him a sense of dread. Through his window, he could see long, sweeping rows of cherry trees in bloom. But this provided no distraction as Emily loved these trees and often spoke about them as being the best part of living in Washington. The wagering man in him allowed that she probably would not live to see them bloom another season. It was consumption, and the coughing would grow stronger and she would grow weaker. She was only 27 years old. But that's the natural order of things, he thought. One did what one did in this world—loved, made war, fought duels, ran for office—and no matter what it was it would not kill you until that summons was served from the Almighty, and then there was nothing one could do to put it off. Andrew had seen it often enough on the battlefield. Some men stood through a hail of gunfire time and again, while others fell from what was nothing more than a shot fired spuriously from the other side. Emily had received her summons. Andrew knew little about medicine, but there was a tone in her cough that was a clear reply to the Almighty. She had served here graciously; he supposed her reward in Heaven would be commensu-

rate. He was grateful to her, but he still missed Rachael, particularly now, during this time of year.

A servant brought dark, bitter coffee—the kind Andrew had discovered in New Orleans—and placed it silently on the desk by the window, then backed out of the room without a word. The staff had learned not to engage him in the morning, when he was at his moody worst. And this was just the sort of morning in which a servant wished to be invisible. They knew him to be adversarial by nature, and this was the time of day when he planned battle strategy. Today would bring another skirmish with Indians, some of the same ones with whom he had marched to Horseshoe Bend, nearly twenty years before. Only now everyone had switched sides. And with Andrew, if you weren't with him, you were against him. This battle would be trickier than others, however. In his mind, he had named it "The Battle of Division and Deception." What irony that one of the same participants who was in his first major battle would be in this one as well!

The Indians had fired the opening volley—a petition to see the President. There were three of them: John Ridge, son of Major Ridge, Elias Boudinot, a young contemporary of Ridge's, and the old chief Junaluska. There was a tangled history between them all. Ridge and Boudinot were the rising leaders of the Cherokee Nation, just beneath the major and John Ross in importance. Jackson had marched to Horseshoe Bend with their fathers. And it was the fathers that Jackson had underestimated years before when friends first became adversaries; he knew that he dared not underestimate them again. That had resulted in a major loss—in bribes and reputation—for him. He was unsure which he resented the most, but the resentment smoldered still. After New Orleans, he almost had a 1.9-million acre tract of Creek land in Alabama in his hands. Then the Cherokees showed up in Washington. At least one of them—Ross, the Principal Chief of the Cherokee Nation—knew how to play the influence game. Ownership of the land had long been disputed by the Creeks and Cherokees. After the Red Sticks were defeated, Jackson had petitioned that the land be awarded to him, as spoils of war for the conquering general. The Cherokees claimed it as theirs, based on an old treaty with the government. But Jackson had put together a new treaty and had it signed by a collection of well-bribed chiefs, giving at least half of the land to him and his friends. He could not lose. But he did. President Madison sided with the Cherokees and the new treaty was nullified.

The land was only part of the rub between these men. In 1830, after the Removal Act had been passed and Ross had subsequently blocked it in the Supreme Court, Jackson had invited him to meet at The Hermitage in Tennessee, to settle this removal matter. It was as close to a peace offering as Andrew had ever made. Ross turned him down, flat.

Ross. Perhaps it was good that he was not going to be here, himself, even though his spirit would surely be in the room. Jackson hated self-important, self-righteous men. It was an instinct that lay in him like a half-submerged alligator and caused his face to redden when he met one. And Ross was every bit of that, even when he had served as Jackson's scribe in the Alabama campaign, embellishing the exploits of the general. Jackson had made him a lieutenant, and remembered that when Ross was going to speak, he would puff himself up, jut out his lip, and ask a sanctimonious question that turned out to be more statement than question. Ross was a climber. What puzzled the President was the path that the man had taken. He was only fractionally Cherokee—by a great grandmother, it was said—and he did not look it at all. His face was European; a shock of wavy hair stood on his head. He could easily pass for merchant or minister. And another thing: He barely spoke the Cherokee language, English with a touch of Scot's burr being much more comfortable for him. So, why had he chosen to be Cherokee when he could have at this point in his life probably been in Congress if he had put himself forward as a White man? Anyhow, the message that would come from this meeting would contain all the feelings that the President had for Ross, even if Ross had to hear them indirectly because the President had denied him an audience.

Something else was forming in his mind that might improve the morning, too. Although the *Worcester vs. Georgia* decision in the Supreme Court had put Indian removal in stalemate and nullified Georgia's attempt to wrest control over the portion of that state that lay across Cherokee land, Jackson thought that he saw a way around it. His plan would require another risk—almost as great as the risk needed to get the Removal Act passed in the first place. Ross and the others had forgotten that he, Jackson, could play the lawyer, too. He had been one for years before the army and politics had pulled him away. Soon after it was decided, Jackson read the *Worcester* decision, line by line. The Chief Justice had allowed that the Cherokee Nation was a sovereign entity, a state within a state. So be it. He had also decreed that their lands could not be taken from them, except by their consent in treaty. One of the things that Jackson remembered from the earlier, aborted treaty, was that some of the

Cherokees were willing to listen to a business proposition. Money got their attention, just as it did any man. Perhaps, he thought, that one of the men who were coming to see him this morning could be convinced to do a deal, if he could find the right rhetoric—and price. If it were possible, he would be able to tell from their eyes. Then, if they were willing and a treaty could be pushed through in a hurry, Jackson would have to go back to congress to get it ratified. He took a deep breath and a sip of coffee. That was the risk. The Removal Act had passed by a single vote. The split in Congress would be similar again. If the treaty were not ratified, the whole removal effort would be dead. But it was the only way to get them out. He just had to find the right Cherokee with whom to deal. And the men were John Ridge, Elias Boudinot, and Chief Junaluska. Around one of them, the shape of the map of the whole country would turn.

Ridge was from North Georgia, a dandy, and perhaps the most important man of the young generation of Cherokees. He was schooled, clever, adaptable. He had amassed considerable wealth and lived on a farm near his father's place in North Georgia. They said that he lived more like a White man than most of the White settlers, attending missionary schools as a boy, holding slaves, and riding like a gentleman with his White wife in a carriage. And, unlike his fellow Cherokees, he dressed like a New England man of the cloth. Perhaps he was the key to breaking the legal logjam on removal, if the President could do business with him. But to do it, Jackson would have to do a hard thing. He would have to take away the young man's hope for a future in Georgia. He would have to continue to let the White settlers make their raids into the Indian territory.

Junaluska. Junaluska was another matter, and a complete contrast to Ridge. Drinking his coffee and watching the sunrise, Jackson remembered that he had not seen Junaluska since Alabama, but he would never forget the man whose face was described as being so broad that it looked like the side of a mountain. He was almost as tall as Jackson, himself, but built much more powerfully—unusual in an Indian. Rangy arms ended at hands that had easily held a ball for the cannons that they had hauled through the piney woods in Alabama. But it was one single image that Jackson most remembered. During battle, the man had moved like a shadow, appearing over Jackson as he lay on the ground, just in time to grab the arm of the Red Stick Creek warrior who was about to bury an axe in Jackson's face. It was an odd struggle as the President recalled it. There had been almost no motion between Junaluska and the Red Stick. Junaluska held the Creek's arm rigidly, eyes locked, then snapped the man's wrist with a sudden twist of his hand. He had never seen such a demonstration of strength. The Creek died quickly and quietly with Junaluska's own axe between his eyes.

Unlike the Ridges, Junaluska was not a rich man, nor did he seem to care about wealth. Junaluska was an aboriginal Cherokee, largely unassimilated by the surrounding White culture. He could speak English passably and he knew enough to follow Ridge's lead when it came to dressing for Washington society. But he lived with his clan in the Snowbird Mountains of North Carolina, a high forbidding place that was almost impassible. The Snowbirds lay next to the line that separated Tennessee from North Carolina, and travelers had long ago learned to avoid them. Unlike North Georgia where Ridge lived, large farms were not successful in the Snowbirds. Families subsisted, but not much beyond that. Junaluska lived there because that was what he knew. Property and slaves meant nothing to him. He did not hold property that he thought of as his own, preferring the older, communal life of the Over Hill Cherokees. And it was said that the people who had made him chief loved him for his old-fashioned ways. Jackson surmised that he would not be easy to approach with a treaty.

What would it take to convince one of these men to turn on the rest? Ridge? Junaluska? Boudinot? Money alone was not motive enough. Jackson needed to break the man's will to resist the removal, to convince him of the futility of holding onto centuries of tradition and give up their ancestral lands. Jackson sensed that he was nearing the point in the struggle with these people where a subtle shift in attitude would determine the outcome of the entire battle. Georgians rode uncontested and unrestricted through Cherokee lands, in search of gold or whatever they could steal. The state was also sending surveyors through the territory, with an eye toward dividing the land and giving it to Whites by lottery. All this must be allowed to continue. Jackson would ignore the Supreme Court and wash his hands of all this, just like Pontius Pilate. He would pretend that nothing was going on . . . that the Cherokees' struggle with the Georgians was a local issue. Then, when the Indians understood that there would be no help, no protection from these settlers who ran through their lands like a pack of hungry hounds . . . then maybe the one man that Jackson was looking for would experience a Judas moment and give in to what was inevitable.

The President recalled their parallel history as he slowly descended a back staircase at the White House.

It was all long ago, but in an irony of fate, the players were gathering again for another battle. It was funny how so many tracks of history had their origins at Horseshoe Bend. That moment began a sequence of events that finally catapulted him into the White House. The Creeks had dug themselves into that position on the bend in the river with the thought that the river, itself, would be their escape route if they needed one . . . Jackson's cannons fired for hours but could not dislodge them . . . but Ridge's sneak attack across the river made the Creeks boil out of their holes like yellow jackets . . . where they were cut down . . . but not before Junaluska had to pull the Red Stick off Jackson . . . and Jackson was written up as the hero . . . by John Ross . . . who would become the Cherokee chief. Shortly thereafter, Horseshoe Bend became New Orleans and Ross became Jackson's nemesis . . . over a land deal that would have perhaps made Jackson the richest man in the South. It was all some twenty years ago.

Coffee in hand, the President settled in his private office where he handled the unseen business of the government. The small room was decorated with memorabilia from Tennessee, a saber that he had carried in New Orleans, shoulder braid from his uniform, a letter declaring him first senator from his home state, a watercolor of his home, The Hermitage. From the single window that looked out over the south lawn, he could see clumps of flowering shrubs, red and white. This was the season of nostalgia for Andrew. It was beautiful here this time of year, and although the time of flowering had passed several weeks before in Nashville, it always reminded him of Rachel, memories that were both so difficult and so necessary. Rachel had loved this season as much as Emily. The faint scent of the flowers never failed to resurrect her image. And it was recollections such as these that sometimes pulled him away from his purpose.

Andrew Jackson was not a man to doubt himself. He did not weigh issues, and he did not toy with ideas. That was one of the reasons that he was not sad to have left the law behind. He could not easily argue a case if the position of the litigant did not inspire passion. When he had served in the Senate, they had said of him that he had been a poor senator because he argued his positions too vociferously, almost violently, and for this he was subject to dialectic entrapment. Well, that was his way. He thought with his guts. And he needed no greater proof of his rightness for the times than the mandate that the people had given him in 1828 and again last year. His was, truly, the most powerful presidency since the first one.

However, as the morning brightened outside, he experienced a moment of ambivalence. Why should he take the added risk of herding these Indians toward a shallow treaty that would eventually lead to their eviction? Certainly, his presidency was at risk if he attempted it. In fact, removal of the Indians would benefit him personally none at all now. He could just as easily relax and let the last three years of his term play themselves out, almost without strife, then retire to The Hermitage and do whatever ex-presidents do. What made him unable to give up the fight? Was it Ross? Was it the land? Or was it just his single-mindedness that once he started on something he could not turn away?

At 10:00 in the morning, the three Cherokee gentlemen were ushered into the President's office. They were dressed in black coats and pants, topped by stiff white collars. Except for the fact that their skin was the color of old copper, they could have been tobacco planters from nearby counties in Maryland. Ridge was the shortest of the three and his face bore both more intelligent and more magnetic qualities. Unlike his father, however, his body was almost delicate, with hair turning in a single curl over his forehead. He smiled tentatively at the President. All three visitors knew that Ridge had reason to be apprehensive. Jackson and Ridge's father had some troubling history between them. They had not met since Jackson served on the commission to settle the Creek land dispute, in 1817. That had gone badly for Jackson, and later, he had been quoted as saying that the Cherokees "stole" the land from him. Also, young Ridge had not forgotten the man's legendary temper, or the fact that everyone knew that, next to Ross, his father was the most responsible for getting that land treaty overturned. But now, Ridge had been approved for this meeting. He was politician enough to sense some kind of shift in the wind of power, however slight.

Ridge stepped forward, hand outstretched and shook the President's hand. "Mr. President, I bring you greetings from an old Chickamaugah warrior."

Jackson half smiled. He must remember to appear reluctant about this meeting. "Welcome to the White House, Mr. Ridge. I trust that your father is well and that you are enjoying your stay in Washington." (Was there too much knowledge implied in his voice? Ridge was known to be a man to make good use of his image as an exotic in the capitol, and not to turn down any invitation.)

"My family is well and, yes, we have been well received." The dapper Indian pulled a piece of polished wood from beneath his coat. "My father sends a gift for an old friend who has risen to be the greatest chief among us."

Jackson accepted the offering, a walnut plaque onto which an image of the State of Alabama was relieved. Around the image was nailed a large horseshoe. At the spot where the Red Sticks had made their stand appeared the date 1814. "Gentlemen, I am pleased." He glanced up to his wall where his old saber hung. "I will find a spot up there to display it."

Jackson turned to Elias Boudinot who was more reserved than Ridge, but who also bore the impression of the White man's culture. "Welcome to the White House, sir."

At that point, Junaluska stepped from behind Ridge and stuck out his hand as he had seen his more polished companions do. Jackson accepted his hand and for a moment they stared at each other eye to eye. In the years since the Alabama campaign, the chief's features had changed from young to old. His skin was weathered like the leather of an old chair, and his hair was now the color of steel. Unlike Ridge, it was obvious that Junaluska lived mostly out of doors. His handshake, however, still spoke of enormous power. From the Indian's point of view, Jackson had changed, too. His always-lean body now seemed frail. Only his eyes held the same intensity as before.

"You do me and this house honor, Chief," the President said.

Junaluska nodded, at first not knowing how to reply. He would speak in council when words were needed, but his people had made him chief more for his mannerisms than his words. Finally, he found something to say. "You were a great warrior, Mr. President. My people remember you as a leader."

Jackson motioned for them to sit opposite his desk. After some talk of battles that they recalled—

Ridge's father had followed Jackson through an ineffectual campaign in Florida while Junaluska had returned to the Snowbirds—Ridge launched into a preamble to their purpose. "My people remain in turmoil, Mr. President. Every day there are encroachments from White settlers onto our lands. They come to seek gold and if they do not find it they take anything that they can. Sometimes they trample our crops. Men have been ambushed. We want peace, but we live in fear."

At this point, his booming voice softened. "We understand your position, sir, on the removal question. But until that is settled, the Cherokees live in a state of siege."

The President sighed and put down a quill that he had been holding. "Where do these . . . incursions come from?"

Both knew who the raiders were, but both knew that they needed to go through the pretense of having it revealed. "Mostly from the settlers in Georgia," replied Ridge.

Jackson nodded. "That does not surprise me. The State of Georgia is a sovereign state and they have a claim to your land that goes back over thirty years, as you well know. The Georgians see that land as theirs. The Supreme Court, on the other hand, has spoken that these lands are to be held separate. As things are now, the matter is not a federal issue. I am not sure what I can do."

Cautiously, Ridge pushed forward an idea that troubled him, even though his father had suggested it before they left for Washington. "Could you not bring back soldiers to stop the raids?"

Jackson kept his face impassive. "Not unless this somehow becomes a federal issue. You need to take the matter up with the Governor of Georgia."

"But he does not listen. Georgia executes our people if we defend ourselves."

Jackson knew all this, but it was a dance of words that had to be danced until it was concluded. "The Supreme Court has decreed that Georgia law is not longer valid in your land."

"They do not listen. They still come," repeated Ridge.

The President almost enjoyed this. The Cherokees were caught in a bind that was largely one of Ross' and the elder Ridge's own making. They strongly advocated nonviolence for their people. So, when the Georgians came on raiding parties, there was no militia or police presence in the Cherokee Nation to repel them. In fact, the Cherokee Nation was no nation at all; it was still nothing more than a collection of tribal clans that shared a tradition of intermarriage. They were a nation on paper only, a myth without an army. Until they formed one, the Georgians and a few of Jackson's fellow Tennesseeans would continue to nip at their territory like horseflies. Jackson enjoyed the image.

"Gentlemen, I don't think that there is anything that I can do for you." He let his words fall heavily in the room.

Tennison's Hotel
Washington, DC
April, 1833

These were days of troubling dreams for Junaluska. Back in his home in the mountains, there was much talk of Cherokee people dreaming dreams that could not be explained. They had come like a plague in the darkness, twisting the sleep of warrior and chief alike. Now they had come to him. What made it worse was that Junaluska was away from his home, in his Snowbird Mountains. He was lying in a strange lodge in the capitol of the White man's government, in a lodge with many rooms, a place that was known as Tennison's Hotel. But the foul cloud of dreams had caught up to him, even here. At night, he tossed on the soft down-filled mattress, and when his eyes closed, he would see a dark sphere of a squirrel's nest outlined in an oak tree, high above him. Perched on the nest was the shape of a large owl, fitfully tearing leaves and bits of twigs from the nest. In his dream, Junaluska felt the remnants flutter down from the tree, over his skin. Once in a while, the owl would stop his assault, cocking his head over the nest to see if the squirrel inside was preparing to escape. When satisfied that his quarry was paralyzed with fear, the owl would commence again.

At this point, Junaluska always woke up. It had been this way for the past three nights. Each night, he felt the terror of the squirrel, but each night the dream ended with no resolution. This time, however, he sat up in bed. He needed to think about what the dream meant.

The problem was that thinking in this place was

difficult. There was no wind in his small room. There were no running streams. There were no birds to hear. And there were too many people and horses and noises of which he did not know the source. He did not believe that an Indian could survive long in this city they called Washington. It distracted and confused his thinking.

Taking what remained of the cigar that the President had given him and lighting it over the flame of an oil lamp, he puffed for a moment. The cigar filled the room with a satisfying smell, but in truth it was the only thing that gave him comfort here. He would have preferred to sleep on the ground outside the White House; after all, there was plenty of room. There were even trees to which they could have tied their horses. But John Ridge would not hear of it. He had said that was not the way people in Washington lived, even Indians. So, here he was, by himself, in this strange room in Tennison's Hotel.

He did not believe that he could do the thinking that he needed to do here. Around the walls were pictures of people whom he did not know. He had asked, but no one in the hotel knew who they were either. They even looked at him peculiarly for asking. Why would White people hang pictures of people whom they did not know? It was a strange custom. There was a fireplace in the room, too. But it was cold and one could not cook over it even if it burned. In the hotel, there were many rooms like his he supposed, more than enough for every family that lived in his village in the Snowbird Mountains. But they would not like it here any more than he did. Almost nothing was how he knew it to be. Not only were the customs strange, the other people in the hotel were too close—too close for a man to do what a man did naturally and not be heard by someone else. Even walking in the hotel was peculiar. The floors were covered by some soft fabric. At first, he was reluctant to walk on it, then he saw Ridge and young Boudinot do it without a second thought, as though it were natural to walk on cloth that bore pictures of birds and clouds. The first thing that he noticed was that his footsteps were as silent as if he were walking through a pine thicket on a deep bed of needles.

He would never get used to it, this White living, not like his two companions. They were the young bloods of the tribe now. Once it had been Junaluska, the Major, and John Ross who were the young bloods. Now, these two were the ones who would carry on. They had even gone to school in a place called New England, where they said snow lay on the ground for much of the year. They had even married White women, both of them. And over the objections of their women, they owned Negro slaves. Just like White men. Just like their fathers.

Junaluska rose from the bed and walked in his nightshirt to a wicker chair beside the window. His black suit hung on a wooden thing that resembled the bones of a man after all the flesh had rotted away. At home, he would have slept in the suit, not in this strange thing that Ridge had given him upon their arrival. White men were very odd, he concluded.

Junaluska sat in the chair, puffing the cigar. Occasionally, a single rider or carriage would pass on the street below. But it was late at night, when most people should be in bed. Even the President would be in bed. As he drew on the cigar, he remembered the first one that Jackson had given him, the one they smoked after the battle in the Creek fortification at Horseshoe Bend. Everywhere, men had been bent to the work of taking trophies from the Creek corpses. Some took ears. Some took tufts of hair. Some tried to skin the warriors with their war paint intact. Jackson watched silently as he walked slowly through the carnage. Junaluska followed him. Killing that Creek who was about to kill the general had made a bond between them, one the White man seemed to have trouble accepting. Abruptly, Jackson stopped walking. He drew a cigar from a pocket inside his uniform. The outer wrapper of brown leaf was broken, probably when he fell. Snapping it in half, he handed one piece to Junaluska and poked the other in his mouth. A stick from a Creek fire provided a light. For a moment, the two men stared at each other with the same probing look that they had shared again in the White House earlier today. Then, Jackson had grinned an acknowledgement of his debt and walked on.

For a moment, the night was still, but it brought no clarity to the dream of the owl and the squirrel. His sense of harmony was gone, stolen by the noise of men snoring down the hall, stolen by the peculiar smell of the soap that White men put on their faces in the morning before they scraped off the hair that grew there, stolen by the endless use of words that had no purpose, stolen by his own need to keep a lamp burning through the night. This was a bad place in which to think. Perhaps, that explained why so many bad ideas had their origin here. People spoke and their words were friendly, but their eyes spoke of other things, sometimes treachery.

White men were not the only ones subject to this peculiar confusion in Washington. It was like a sickness. When they came here, the Cherokees could become infected, too. He had noticed it in his companion, John Ridge. At dinner the night before—an invitation arranged by Ridge in the home of a Massachusetts congressman—Ridge had put on the face of what Junaluska could only describe as an Indian dignitary . Indians did not have dignitaries. They had chiefs. Junaluska would have been happier if John Ridge had acted more like a chief. But, his speech became increasingly flowery as wine flowed, bottle after bottle. He proclaimed a growing bond between Whites and Indians, a joining in Christian brotherhood, a sharing of common purpose. He swept on for long minutes at a time, like the great gusts of summer storms that rolled over the Snowbirds. Junaluska had never heard such words, certainly not from an Indian. As he spoke, Ridge would emphasize his points with sweeps of his arms. Junaluska sat silently throughout the oration.

The morning before they went to see the President, Ridge had seemed himself again. Perhaps, it had been the wine; it was known to be poisonous to Indians. But something had taken place in the White House to make Ridge a stranger again.

After explaining that he could do nothing to ensure their domestic protection, the President had risen abruptly, signaling that their interview was over. After shaking hands again, the three Cherokees were ushered to the door. But just as they stepped outside, the President's secretary rushed up and called Ridge back inside. Junaluska and Boudinot waited outside, near a large white column, watching as a sparrow built a nest within the curl of the capital. It took a long time for Ridge to return. He came out and rushed past his companions as though he had forgotten that they were waiting. Realizing his error, he turned and in an un-Indian way, began to fidget.

Junaluska knew that he had to leave Washington. This place turned good men mad, like the dogs that shake in the summer. Indians simply did not . . . fidget. He could not make himself say the word.

Back at the hotel, Junaluska announced to Boudinot and Ridge that he was going home. Ridge tried to draw him to another dinner, but the look from the taller man told him that he had had enough of strange foods and strange customs. He yearned for the simplicity of his wife's kettle. To be comfortable again, he needed the smoke of a dinner fire to saturate his clothes and the intrusions of his dog trying to steal a scrap of food. Maybe back in the Snowbirds he would find out why the owl was destroying the squirrel's nest.

Nantahala River
Cherokee Nation
Early May, 1833

The Nantahala River never ran warm, but in the spring it held the sharp bite of winter longer than any river that Tsali knew. Perhaps, it was even colder than the Oconaluftee that was always brutally cold. As he worked the fish trap near his cabin, he felt his aging legs begin to go numb. He would have to take the fish quickly while he could, before his feet refused his commands to move. But the take would be good today, worth the torment of cold. Dark green forms swirled and darted with panic in the upper part of the trap, the part where they entered gradually as they swam upstream, but were unable to escape. There was enough for him and his wife and some for their grown children who lived nearby. Tsali scooped into the trap with a basket that was woven from thin canes of the bamboo that grew in unyielding thickets beside the river. Water passed easily through the wide weave, but any fish that was big enough to eat could not. More than a dozen flopped desperately as he raised the basket out of the water. Good ones. There were three with a speckled swath of gold on their sides, four with the long lateral black stripe that ran the length of their bodies, three round ones with the spot of gold under their mouths, and two large ugly ones with their mouths turned down. They were bottom feeders and bony. Sometimes, Tsali tossed them back because they were hard to eat, but Nancy knew how to make a stew of them that was good, so this time he decided to leave them in the basket.

Tsali was thinking about dinner when he looked

up and was surprised by a man on horseback. That the man was Indian was clear—his hair and eyes were very dark—but from his clothes, Tsali could not tell which kind of Indian he was. For a moment, he felt a different kind of chill. The man was dressed more formally than any White man, except those preachers who roamed the mountains now, jabbering and praying, and trying to convert the Indians to the White man's religion. Tsali hoped that he was not a preacher. If he were, he did not want to listen to him. Religion was one of the White man's things for which he had no use. The Great Spirit was just that. A man lived, used what he needed until he died and his four souls dispersed. There was no need to say more. He had heard some of the preacher talk from his neighbors. It was strange and it confused him. He hoped that this man on horseback was not a preacher.

The man got down and waited, bridle in hand, as Tsali eased out of the river. "You have a good catch," he said, observing the obvious.

Tsali nodded. While the stranger was clearly Indian, his manners were White. No Indian would come upon another unannounced unless he intended to steal something. But this man's manner and looks spoke no harm. He was oddly delicate for a Cherokee, and wore his hair pushed up on top of his head. He did not seem like a man who worked for a living. Tsali decided to wait to see what he wanted, hoping it was not this thing the preachers said was his only soul.

"I am of the Chickamaugah, from near New Echota. I am called John. You may know my father, Kahnungdatlageh, who is also known as Major Ridge."

Tsali settled the basket of fish in the grass beside the river. He had heard of this place—New Echota—but had never seen it. It was said that a

Cherokee named Ross had built a town there, just like a White man's town. It was where the council met. Maybe they made more trouble there than they were worth. That was all he knew. "I have heard of this place," Tsali said.

Without hesitation, the son of Kahnungdatlageh began to speak. "The government in Washington wants all the Indians—the Cherokees, the Creeks, the Seminoles, the Chickasaws, and the Choctaws—to leave their homelands and move west to a new place called Oklahoma. You know of this?"

Tsali grunted loudly enough so that it was audible above the sound of the river. "I know that there has been talk of White men taking this land since my sons came of age. It makes the people afraid. Sometimes they are so afraid that they forget to plant. But we are still here."

John eased back in his boots as though he were gathering himself. "We are here because our stubbornness has resisted the attempts of the government and White settlers in Georgia and a few in Tennessee to make us leave. We have fought well and even had one part of the government—the Supreme Court—say that we could stay. But stubbornness alone will not hold this for us. It appears that those against us are relentless. The President, himself, has turned his back on us."

Tsali sat on a fallen tree, resting his legs. The cold scent of the river contrasted with the warm bath of sun that fell on him. A dragonfly moved cautiously between the two men. "What do you want of me? I am only who I am, what you see. I know nothing of these things."

The slender man pulled a sheath of papers from his coat, unfolded them, and held them up before

Tsali. There were pages of black marks, followed by pages of lines on which a few other marks—some of them in dark blue—appeared. "This is a treaty that we make with the government in Washington. For giving them all this land that we live on now, they will give us much land in the West where there is no one to raid and steal our property. It is called the Treaty of New Echota."

Tsali stared at the script. The regular up-and-down lines of writing had always mystified him. Some men, he knew, put great store in this. He did not know why. "I do not read," he said simply.

The younger man replaced one set of papers with another. "These are in Cherokee."

"I do not read those, either."

The man named John was frustrated. "I would like to explain this to you. Is there someplace where we can sit and talk?"

Tsali nodded toward the southerly slope of the mountain behind John. "My cabin is there, in a cove. I will send my grandson to fetch his father and uncles who are nearby. If you will eat these fish with us, you can explain your treaty to all of us. None of them read, either."

The two made their way along a small stream that tricked into the river. John walked his horse and followed. The cabin was small, dug into the bank of the mountain. The ground on the rising approach was worn smooth by the comings and goings of people. Even the roots that ran from the maples that shaded the house were polished by frequent passage of moccasins.

A boy of perhaps a dozen years watched unmoving as they approached. Only when he saw the old man laboring with the basket of fish did he move to help, but his eyes never left the stranger.

"Get your father and uncles," Tsali said, and the boy disappeared. "That is my grandson," he explained. "He is called Wasseton."

A woman with gray hair pulled into a tight bun emerged from the cabin. She looked without expression from one man to another. "This man has come to us from the Chickamaugah. He has a new treaty that he will read to us. His name is John and he is the son of Kahnungdatlageh."

Over the afternoon, Tsali's two sons, named Canantutlaga and Lau in nih, arrived, as did his daughter and her husband. Each brought their own families, with children as young as five. The children stared openly at John. Not only was he a stranger, but he had a White man's clothing and bearing. He was not an Indian who was accustomed to sitting cross-legged around a fire and rolling his bread between his fingers before he ate it. This was a "table Indian," perhaps schooled in the Christian schools that it was said the Chickamaugah favored. He could not be more unlike Tsali and his family if his skin were white. But he was Cherokee, like them.

As evening drew near, dark night-like shadows began to cover the lower portion of the valley. Even next to patches of sunlight, they were cold and mysterious as though they held secrets or sickness. The family ate the fish quietly, on the ground, in front of the cabin. Even though they had eaten their grandfather's fish many times, the flesh was special to the children and it showed in their faces. John ate with them, looking mildly out of place.

When they were done, they looked at John and waited. Once again, he took out the papers in his black coat and flattened them with his hand. When he read, he did so slowly, allowing each phrase to be understood before he went on.

The treaty spoke of how the Cherokees would sell their land to the government and would collectively be moved to a new homeland in the Territory of Oklahoma, where there was already a small settlement of Cherokees who had gone there over a dozen years before. Each family would have its own farm and the tribe would be given $5 million in exchange for the land left behind.

He described how the people would leave the Cherokee Nation and migrate in a large group to the West. They might go by boat on the Tennessee River, or they might go overland by wagon train. When he was done, he showed them the pages of blank lines for their signatures. There were not many marks on these lines. "Will you sign this and come with the Chickamaugah to the West?" he asked, trying to hide the plea in his voice and sound more like a Cherokee.

No one answered at first. They all waited on Tsali, or Nancy, if she chose to speak. But it was Tsali, as expected, who replied. "You bring us thoughts that are not easy. As a man, myself, I would like to see a new land. If I were like my sons and still a young man, I would think that I would like to see it. They say that there are still buffalo to be hunted there, and, I am told, great herds of horses. That would be a story to tell my people. To chase a horse instead of a deer would be a great hunt.

"But I am old and I know my years are few. Perhaps, I would not survive the journey, as my legs are not as good as those of a young man. And this valley has been good to me, as it was to the family of my wife who allowed me to come here to live, from the Oconaluftee where I was born. When I die, my body will become part of this land, and my spirit will come here to sit beside the river to remember all the fish that I took and ate. How can I leave a place of which I am part?"

John answered quickly, too quickly for politeness. "The Whites will drive you out. They will take your land. They will take your cabin. They will even take your fish trap. I have seen them. Where they come, they take. And the government will not stop them. They will come in twos and tens, and they will have guns. I know of farmers who have had their women dragged into the woods and beaten by one bunch while their horses were stolen by another. Already, in Georgia, they have parties of men traveling through with things they call survey instruments, and they divide up the land—my land—on pieces of paper to wait for the day when they can give it to their friends. This, too, will happen here. By signing the treaty, it means that we get something in return for what we will inevitably lose."

"Can we not fight them?"

"We have. But they are many. We are few. And we do not act like a nation. We act like what we are—a group of families—who live on a big land and are suspicious of each other. And they know that about us."

"And you say that the White government will not help us?"

John nodded. "The President, himself, told me so."

Tsali rose from the ground. All eyes in the circle of fire watched him. He stood with his back to them, a hand resting on the trunk of an old maple. "I do not know if I can do this thing that you ask. Rest here tonight. Continue on your journey to the other people in the valley and along the Tuckasegee. Return in two weeks and I will give you my decision."

The next day, when Tsali saw the Chickamaugah's horse disappear from view, he went into his cabin and took down a bag with a leather strap. His wife watched him as he packed corn meal and some dried venison. This woman, with whom he had lived since he was barely a man, knew instinctively where he was going. "Pack something warm. Perhaps, your hunting coat. It is still cold in the Snowbirds," she advised.

This time of year, it was almost two day's walk to the high mountain village where his friend Junaluska lived. The trail along the Nantahala was easy going, but when the river turned south, he continued west, climbing slowly to a pass. Then, he circled the knob of another mountain and headed northwest. He did not have to think about where he was going. His moccasin-covered feet held fast to the trail that was wet in spots with springtime seepage. Stopping by a rock that dripped cold water, he took a handful and drank. It tasted faintly of the moss that grew like a collar around the rock. Standing still now, he listened as the forest came alive. There were sounds of chipmunks and sparrows.

Tsali looked northwest along a connected line of mountains. He would walk the trail on the southeast flank until he reached a pass between two peaks. Then he would descend steeply along a small stream that would eventually lead, with much walking, to Junaluska's village. A cold wind came at his face and he was glad that he had heeded Nancy's advice and carried his hunting coat. Lifting the bag, he walked on.

By late afternoon, he reached the saddle in the

mountains where he could look westerly, toward the Snowbird range. The sun rested in the peaks beyond and would soon be gone. The wind had died, but there were clouds around the sun. If the wind picked up again, he did not want to be sleeping here so he hurried down the mountain.

At dark, Tsali came to a small clearing that had been caused by a fire from lightning, two or three years before. A clump of broom sage had sprung up and provided a soft place to lay. He broke the stalks into a mat and was asleep by the time darkness was complete.

A crow woke him in the morning, with a loud cawing. There was no sleeping past that. It reminded Tsali of an old chief from his boyhood along the Oconaluftee. He, too, had made more noise than was necessary, and inevitably people wondered why they had made him chief. Tsali smiled inwardly at the memory. It was good to think of something that made him want to smile. There was not much of that these days. Most of the happenings that came to his ears were dark, troubling, like this John of the Chickamaugah. What would Junaluska say about John Ridge? He rose. It would be afternoon before he reached the village.

The Snowbird Clan lived along the Cheoah River and two lesser streams that flowed into it. Not as big as the Nantahala, it raced between dark boulders that defined the bank. A collection of forty log cabins were scattered along the valley that was shaped like a bowl. In the afternoon sun, Tsali found Junaluska kneeling beside the river, washing dirt from a pile of wild garlic that he had dug in the woods. Whatever dinner was tonight, it would have much flavor.

Tsali called to him from across the river.

Junaluska rose and waved to his friend, then pointed to a jagged line of rocks that served as a passage across the water. When Tsali was on the other side, they clutched each other's forearms, as was the Cherokee custom.

"You are a long way from your lodge," Junaluska chided.

"I come with news, and a question," the older man replied.

"Ah, then you have not just come for my wife's cooking?"

"It would be worth the journey. But, no, I am in need of your understanding."

Junaluska assessed his visitor. He could not remember when they did not know each other. Although Tsali had felt too old to go on the campaign with him and Andrew Jackson to Alabama, he had been the first from outside Junaluska's village whom he had asked. Their shared respect was familial in its nature.

"Come, let's get away from the noise of this river and you can speak of your news."

The two men settled on a flat rock not far from Junaluska's cabin. His wife, a woman of some years herself, waved to them from the doorway, but did not approach. Many times she had enjoyed a gift of Tsali's fish, but this did not appear to be one of those times. This was something else, from the look of them. Junaluska picked up a small limb, and with his skinning knife, began to whittle aimlessly. It was his signal that he was ready to listen to the story of his friend.

Tsali began cautiously. "I have hunted these mountains and fished these rivers since before I have memory," he said, sweeping his arm along the horizon.

"It has been a good life. In spring, we plant, just as you do here. When the leaves change to red, we harvest and dance. If there is trouble between us, we speak about it until harmony is found. It is all that I know.

"Two days ago, a man the age of my sons came to me from the Chickamaugah and said that I should sign this paper that would end our life here. His name was John Ridge and he is the son of Kahnungdatlageh. He said that you know him. This paper would give us another place to live, a place far to the west that I have never heard of. He said that there would be a farm for each man, and much money. I could tell that he wanted me to sign the paper.

"I thought to do this thing that he asked, but I could not see how to leave here."

Junaluska took a deep breath. "What did you tell him?"

"I told him to go away and come back in two weeks . . . that I would think on it."

"Could you do this thing that he asks?"

Tsali rubbed his hand along the rock where he sat, brushing softly over a patch of moss. "I do not see how. I am of this," he said, patting the rock. "The Chickamaugah live another way. I could not tell this man from a White man, although his skin was almost as dark as mine." He paused, then finished what he had to say. "How could I become something else?"

Junaluska rocked back where he sat. "All the settlers want us to go, especially those in Georgia. Even my old friend, the President, betrays us. At first, they just wanted our land. Now, they want the gold that they say is in it. It is said that the Creeks will be leaving soon. We are on our own."

"What will happen?"

With the stick that he had sharpened, Junaluska scratched at the dirt between his feet. "John Ross says that we can hold on, even though they have taken his own lands in Georgia. We have won the case in the Supreme Court in Washington. They cannot force us to go unless we sign a treaty giving them the right to move us off."

Abruptly, Junaluska stood up with a puzzled look. "My friend, you have brought me a gift."

It was Tsali's turn to be puzzled. "I brought you nothing, only this news."

Junaluska raised his hand. "Forgive me. You could not understand. You see, I have had a dream that has haunted my sleep. For months, I have consulted the elders here, but no one could explain it. I even went to a place in the mountains that is holy for me, and waited for the spirits to explain the dream. But it was not explained. But, just now, my friend, you have explained it."

Tsali still did not understand, so Junaluska described his dream about an owl that tore into the nest of a squirrel. "At first, I thought that the owl might have been Andrew Jackson, or even the settlers from Georgia. But now I know that the owl is John Ridge and we are the squirrel's nest."

The two men were silent for so long that the sound of the river reemerged, splashing far in the distance. Finally, Tsali announced, "I cannot sign his paper."

"You will not be asked to again. He will not be back. He will find no interest in the people of the Nantahala, or Tuckasegee, or Oconaluftee to leave. What could be better than what they have now? So, he will go home and try to find enough people around New Echota to sign his paper."

Both considered this for a moment. "What will become of us?" Tsali wondered.

"Maybe nothing. Maybe everything. But it is my belief that whatever happens is out of our hands."

Later, the two shared a dinner of rabbit stew with Junaluska's wife, then as they sat before a fire in front of Junaluska's cabin, other men from the village approached and took a seat. Some came to listen; others put in a word when something came to mind. Junaluska repeated Tsali's news about the proposed treaty, and that the man from New Echota was urging their neighbors to sign it. Consensus among those gathered was that no one would sign it. But later, as they drifted off to their own lodges to sleep, this thought brought little comfort.

Tsali slept in Junaluska's cabin on a bed of straw. It was deeper than the one that he had pushed together the night before. But the softness of the bed did not prevent his own recurring dream from returning. The dog was there, teeth bared, followed by the soldier in a dark uniform, riding and weeping in the rain.

When he awoke, Junaluska was standing just outside the open door, looking over his village. Tsali could not see his face, but there was a sadness about him. Without turning, Junaluska spoke, "Yesterday, you said that you bore news and a question. What was your question?"

Tsali rose and stepped outside. "I had heard of your dream. The people speak of it. I, too, had a dream." He explained about the dog that turned on its master and the weeping rider. "It comes to me, over and over. Can you tell me what it means?"

Junaluska pondered the image for a time, then shook his head. "There is something familiar about it—as though it does not surprise me that this dream has come to you—but I cannot tell you the meaning of it."

Tsali nodded. "What will you do now?"

"I must take this news of yours to John Ross. If anything can be done to save this squirrel's nest of ours, he is now the only one who can do it."

Ross Landing
Cherokee Nation
Late May, 1833

The little stream that would eventually feed the Tennessee River moved by slowly. Dark water swirled in easy circles behind a cluster of smooth pieces of flint that lay near the bank. John Ross had been staring at it, for how long he did not remember. He was worried. The long journey to Washington had not gone well, but he honestly did not know why. The obvious problem was there: His people remained threatened, their future uncertain. A month before, his own lands in Georgia had been confiscated and given to a White settler while he had been in Washington. He returned to find his wife, Quatie, and his children being "allowed" to stay in two rooms of the house until he showed up to take them away. The noose around the Cherokees was growing tighter. They had been fighting Georgian usurpation of their lands for twenty years. A whole generation had grown up thinking that the next Green Corn Festival that they celebrated might be their last.

The focus of Ross' thinking always returned to one man: Andrew Jackson. Without Jackson, Ross knew that he could keep Georgia at bay until they grew weary of their pursuit of land. Except for Jackson. Andrew Jackson was still—always—in a vindictive mood and had refused to see him while he was in Washington. The Jackson he had come to know over the years was a mean, small-minded man who fed off retribution. One only had to recite the list of his duels for proof. Ross wondered why he had expected Jackson to be different as President than he had been as a publicity hungry general, land speculator, poser.

But it was not what he knew about Jackson that troubled Ross. Maybe it was what he did not know. Jackson was capable of anything. Alabama had taught him that. The general had gone after the Red Stick Creeks a month after he had taken a bullet in the arm in a duel. For what? For glory. For reputation. For—eventually—power. Early in his career, Jackson had been a flop as a senator. Becoming a general was a way to remake himself. So, he had coaxed a military appointment from the Governor of Tennessee and led an untrained, undisciplined army against the Red Sticks. He had almost failed, except for Major Ridge's plunge into the river to steal the Red Sticks' canoes. Had the outcome of that one action determined the future for all of them?

Now, years later, Jackson and Ridge stuck in Ross' mind again. He had no evidence of anything to provoke worry, except for the rumor about those two pups of Ridge's who now seemed to be wavering about removal. It was said that the younger Ridge and his cousin Elias Boudinot argued to cut a deal and sell out. They would move the tribe west, as Jackson wanted. But the Supreme Court had blocked the Removal Act. The Cherokees were declared a nation unto themselves, and could not be removed unless they signed a treaty agreeing to it—which no member of the tribe in their right mind would do. Thus, they were free to become whatever they wanted to become. So, why was he worried?

Ross rose on stiff knees and thought about Washington. Something had taken place there when Junaluska had accompanied young Ridge and Boudinot there, perhaps something ominous. They had been admitted to the White House, and afterward

Junaluska reported that Jackson refused to help keep the Georgians out of Indian land. After they returned from seeing the President, Junaluska left Washington abruptly. Junaluska was not a man to hide his thoughts, but Ross speculated that he had been hiding something when he mounted his enormous gray horse and rode west, back to the Snowbirds. Ridge and Boudinot stayed behind.

As a nation, the Cherokees appeared secure. But settlers in Georgia were becoming increasingly aggressive. Those around the five northwestern Georgia counties made naked incursions into the nation, stealing cattle, hogs, even corn meal. Two Cherokees had been shot in the back, from ambush. There were regular raids into the Dahlonega area—not far from Ridge's own plantation—by prospectors searching for gold. These provoked more violence. Yet, Jackson had pulled federal troops out two years ago, denying them protection. At first, this had seemed like a victory to Ross, getting rid of the federal presence. Now, he was not so sure.

So, where was Major Ridge on all this? For months, Ross had heard nothing from the stout man whose face reminded people of a bull. The two of them had come far together. For years, they had been the two loudest critics of the older generation of chiefs, scolding them for failing to keep tribal lands and customs intact. They had been friends, friendly competitors when Ross was elected Principal Chief, then friends again. Ross often sat impassively in council as Ridge spoke for him, being better with the Cherokee language. A kind of teamwork developed between them, the chief and his mouthpiece, with Ridge presenting and Ross presiding . Others in the Cherokee council grew to expect it. The interplay went way back with them, before 1828 when Ross was elected Chief. It was there as they developed the format and arguments for the Constitution of the Cherokee Nation, it was there in the Constitution Convention in 1827. It was there as they formulated ideas for the Cherokee capital in New Echota. Theirs was a political marriage in which both thrived. For men who thought of themselves as Cherokee, talk between them was, atypically, constant. It had seemed necessary. There was much to do. They took the flood of ideas that washed over them from White encroachment—from the government, from Indian agents, from settlers living on their borders, from the Moravian missionaries—and translated each wave for the Cherokees. Sometimes, they spent hours around a fire, developing strategies to resist White ideas that were inimical to Cherokee interests. In spite of the anxiety that he felt constantly now, Ross knew that they had done well for their people, he and Ridge. They had formed their own nation out of a confederacy of clans, written its constitution, established its capitol, published its newspaper. But perhaps the most important thing that they had done was to alter the perception in the minds of the millions of Whites who surrounded them, from that of tribe to nation . Then they had tested their concepts in the U.S. Supreme Court—just as Whites in any civil dispute would have done—first losing, but then coming back again to gain a great victory that would prevent removal. Now, within the Cherokee Nation, their people were allowed wide latitude in how they lived. Some, such as Junaluska of the mountain clans, could live as they always did, with their small farms and hunting. Others, such as the middle and lower clans, could live and prosper much as the White settlers did. Ross was not ashamed that he had been a wealthy man.

Schools founded by missionaries flourished. Tolerance prevailed, jealously was discouraged. They were all Cherokee here, even him. It was good what he and Ridge had done.

But Ridge had been silent in Georgia for almost a year. Even the confiscation of Ross' own property in Georgia after he returned from Washington had brought no word from Ridge. Ross had fled to Tennessee to escape the Georgians, and built a small cabin near the river. But there had been no word from Ridge. Perhaps, he suffered a fever. Perhaps, it was something else. Perhaps, he did not like it last year when Ross rebuked his son, John, over the issue of ceding land. Now, Ridge was silent. What message lay in the silence?

Ross stood up from where he had been sitting beside the stream. Water spiders played a darting game along the edge, and reflections of fading sunlight on the surface shimmered like a golden film. The Indian in him followed the course of the current both ways in his mind. West, beyond the wide bend where he stood, it turned northerly into the hills. Eventually, it would wind its way back southwest, through the land that they had taken from the Creeks—and Andrew Jackson—where it would widen and slow even more. Upstream, where it was shallow, tribe members built fish traps from sticks and rocks and fed their families from what they caught.

He was proud of his people, and felt privileged to be allowed among them, let alone be their elected leader. These were, mostly, good people, simple people, but people who were collectively wise enough to know that an upheaval lay over the horizon for them. Perhaps, Ross reflected, that is why they made him chief. They understood that he, himself, was not even legally an Indian. But they also understood that he just might be White enough to keep the Whites out of their land. Maybe it was lucky for Ross and the rest of them that old Chief Doublehead had been such a thief in the sale of tribal lands to the Georgians. Maybe it was luck, too, that Ridge had shot him. That way, the Cherokees could accept Ross, a reformer, as Chief. That way, they would accept him, even thought he was not legitimately Cherokee.

A tinkling sound from the stream caught his attention. In an eddy current near the bank, a small glass bottle bounced between rocks. Ross was not given to believing in signs, a fact that he did not willingly reveal to his adopted people because signs and omens and dreams were powerful messages to them. But the tinkling bottle stopped him. "Even here," he said to no one, "the tribe of my grandfather invades the tribe of my grandmother."

The sound jarred him back to the present. Omens and dreams, it was something like that which brought on his present mood. If he were back in his grandfather's Scotland, he might have roamed the moors in search of what troubled him. As it was, he walked beside the creek, alone. His wife, Quatie, had seen him leave the cabin and knew him well enough not to follow. She knew the look of tribal business.

It was tribal business that stuck in his gut like bad meat. Junaluska had sent a messenger to say that he would arrive within the week to visit the Chief. Junaluska did not leave the high Snowbirds without reason. He was uncomfortable in the low lands of the Middle Towns in Tennessee and Georgia. He had hated Washington, although he had not said so. And he liked these low rolling hills in the Tennessee only slightly better. Junaluska was and always would be a completely aboriginal Cherokee. He was a humble man, one who spoke more of his failures than triumphs, but his own clan revered him. He moved like a large cat through the woods, and Ross had seen his strength with his own eyes at Horseshoe Bend. Junaluska was not a man with whom one trifled. And he was coming to see Ross because of a dream. The messenger had quoted the cryptic words: "I know why the owl tears at the nest of the squirrel."

Today, there would be answers. The man on horseback rode toward him with dignity. From far away, Ross could tell that it was Junaluska. Hatless, his bearing was upright. He rode slowly, with purpose, as though his purpose carried him as much as the big gray horse beneath him. When his features were close enough to be recognized in the dying twilight, Junaluska began the traditional shouted greeting. The horse came forward, head low as though it understood the serious mission of its rider. From the edge of the water, Ross raised his hand in greeting. He tried to smile, but the look on Junaluska's face stopped him. Indeed, he brought answers.

They spoke of family and ate the evening meal inside the cabin, Ross, his wife Quatie, and Junaluska. A somber politeness hung in the air. When finished, Junaluska nodded thanks to the woman, and the men stepped outside. She understood that it was tribal business again, and did not like the look of it.

When the two reached the stream, they put sticks together for another fire, and then Ross went back inside the cabin to retrieve some glowing embers. It took a few minutes, but soon the flames began to rise between the sticks of sycamore. The light spread across the surface of the water, opening a cavern in the darkness.

"I did not understand about the owl," Ross said, starting the exchange.

Junaluska grunted. "You could not. It was a dream that came to me again and again, even when we were in the White capital. It came every night. I saw an owl, and the owl was tearing at the nest of a squirrel. It seemed that the owl was patient, but that it was determined to get the squirrel. Pieces of the nest fell from the tree and fell onto me." He shook his head. "I could not understand, even though I thought on it for many nights."

Again, he paused, collecting his ideas. "When I returned to the Snowbirds, I went to a place that is sacred for me, a saddle in the mountains between two peaks. There is a wind that comes through it from the west, and many things are revealed within the wind. I went there before I chose my wife, and again before we went with Ridge and his Chickamauga Clan into Alabama to fight the Creeks. It is 'The Place of Truth' for me."

Junaluska rose to gather sticks that had washed up on the bank. When he returned, he set several into the fire, their damp ends sizzling. "I sat there for some days, I do not know how many. The smoke of my fire blew over me and I thought that the spirit of the wind would make the dream known to me. I sat there until my wife became worried and sent someone for me. Still, the answer did not come. I went home, unable to understand."

Ross was tempted to intervene with questions, but he resisted the impulse. With all his self-control, he would try to smother his impatience. As a boy, he had learned that a story was like life, itself; it had a birth, a middle age, and an end. To interrupt was to stop the process and be rude.

"When I returned home, I wandered around, not knowing what to do. I consulted the wisest men of my village, but all that they could tell me was that they would think on it. None of them had an answer.

"Then, one day a man came asking for me, he was an old man, older than me, a friend of many years. He had come all the way from the Nantahala, because he had heard that I had a dream that I could not understand, and because he had had a visitor."

"Could he tell you the meaning?" Silently, Ross chastised himself for interrupting.

"No. He came because he, too, had had a dream. But in his dream, a dog turned and attacked his master, and there was a soldier on horseback, weeping. That's all that I know."

"Why did he seek you out?"

Junaluska put more sticks on the fire, carefully arranging each as though doing so might somehow give order to his thoughts. "He said that his dream might be connected to his visitor. This visitor was a young man who said that I was known to him. He brought the old man a paper and told him that he wanted him to sign it. The old man—he is called Tsali—told the visitor that he could not read, could not even read the Cherokee words. The young man explained that the paper was a new treaty with the Great Father in Washington. He said nothing more. Then Tsali told him that he would have to think about this treaty. It was then that he came to see me."

"Who was this young man?"

"He told Tsali that he was the son of the great chief of the Chickamauga, The One Who Walks the Ridge."

A cold chill overcame Ross, as though he had

learned of a pending death in his family. Aye, he thought to himself, this will cause many deaths. So, it was young Ridge who turned and let in this wolf, this cancer on the tribe. For a long time he sat beside the water with Junaluska, staring at the fire. Abruptly, he looked up at the old chief of the Snowbirds. "John Ridge is your owl," he said quietly.

Near New Echota
Georgia
December, 1835

At the age of 60, Major Ridge realized that he was not too old to learn something new. The 350 men camped around his farm and in the woods between his farm and New Echota were there to conclude what they all knew to be the best of a bad deal. The task within their task was to find the means of living with the decision that they were about to make. Ridge had never made such a bargain with himself. As a young warrior, he learned quickly that one killed or was killed. No weighing the decision was necessary. Even when he had killed Chief Doublehead, it was a thing that needed doing. Doublehead certainly deserved to die, thief that he was. No debate was involved. Later, after he had learned the White man's business of trading and how to strike a deal, he spent no time anguishing over his commitment. But anguish had come to him now, and he was going to have to learn to breathe around a large, tight knot that seemed permanently lodged in his chest.

Unlike many of his fellow Cherokees, Ridge slept with no dreams now. Although he needed them as he needed water, dreams had abandoned him, leaving a vacuum in his head where he had expected the voices of his father and his grandfather. Where had their wisdom gone? It was different in the old days. One just knew how things would be and how they would turn out. On the night before Horseshoe Bend, he and his force of Cherokees listened to the sounds of dancing from the Creek camp that drifted across the river.

The Creeks sensed that the attack would come in the morning and opened themselves to the spirits, in preparation of what was to come. Andrew Jackson ordered his party to be silent, so the Cherokees had no opportunity for their own dancing and singing. Instead, the spirits had come to them in dreams. That night, Ridge tossed and fought with creatures that attacked from both sides. By morning, he felt purified for battle.

What was revealed to Ridge now came from his son, John. The old major trusted John, he loved John like no other person, he promoted John within the tribe, going so far as to have him named Translator to the Council. John's future had become the old man's remaining purpose. But now it felt peculiar to take direction from him. It was John who had met with the President two years before, who brought back the concept that Jackson was going to do nothing while the Georgians simply picked their bones clean. His words were, "The President pretends that Worcester vs. Georgia never occurred. We have no protection. They will consume us when they learn that the gate is open and there will be no federal troops to stop them." Elias Boudinot had been with him at the White House and confirmed the impression. The Cherokees, as a people, had better make the best deal that they could, while they could.

A deal. It all came down to a deal, their lives and traditions bargained in a deal. The major rose from a ladder-back rocker beside his fireplace and walked to the window that overlooked the front of his plantation. All around, there were forms asleep on the ground. He knew that they slept there for his protection. His oldest and dearest friend, John Ross, would have him shot if he could, before this treaty was signed. After today, it would make no difference. Their business here—even their history—was concluded. The Georgians had won. The Treaty of New Echota was the best deal that they were going to get. Later today, the major would put his signature to it.

Quietly, Ridge opened the front door of the grand house that he had built in the rolling hills of North Georgia. Beyond the fine pillared porch lay a stretch of grass, now dormant in the December chill. Here and there, a few fires put columns of smoke into the still dawn air. A gray haze of frost lay on the grass. The men who had slept close to his house had slept cold, the major concluded. He was grateful for their presence. Because of them, John Ross would not come.

Ross would not be here today, for the signing. Principal Chief Ross would stay in his lair in Tennessee, across the Coosa River. The treaty would never have his blessing, because it was not his.

Ridge signed. He was tired in a way that had nothing to do with being old, but it made him feel the accumulation of years. He was tired of the struggle that he and his people had endured for a generation. He was tired of the ever heightening sense of outrage as the White settlers of Georgia conceived of some new, and until then, unthinkable atrocity to steal their land. He was tired of trying to convince Ross and the others in Tennessee and North Carolina that there was no longer any point to holding on to what they had, that it was going to be grabbed from them anyhow. He was tired of seeing no future here for his son and grandchildren. Life could go on, perhaps, in this new place that the government in Washington offered. But it could not go on here or they would all be killed. He was tired of the anger that swept over him at the idea of some settler with a gloating, superior attitude living in the house that he, Major Ridge, had built. Yes, he was tired and almost ready to leave. Almost.

Descending the flagstone steps from his porch, Ridge moved into the frozen grass. He walked slowly, hands in the pockets of a canvas coat, with no discernible purpose. Past the split-log barns and sheds and slave quarters behind the house, he eased into the orchard that lay on a slow-rising hill. Rows of trees stood bare against the early sky. There were hundreds of them, silent, waiting for the energy of spring to bring them back to life. Ridge laid his hand on one after another, touching them as he would an old friend. He had planted them—many with his own hands—but he would not see them bloom again. By the time the buds were out, a White Georgian would be living in his house and watching the progress of the peaches and apples. Perhaps, John would plant trees where they were going. The major was too old to do so himself. He wondered if peaches grew in Oklahoma.

Who was the man who would follow him here? Ever since John and Elias had come back downcast from Washington, the major had been haunted by the face of a man whom he did not know. When no one was around or as he sat by his fire or as he watched the beehive of activity around the farm, he tried to picture the face of the man who would take his place. Which man with whom he had probably traded would sit out the rest of the winter beside the major's fire, eat honey harvested last fall on cornbread baked from corn grown in the field south of the house? He would just move in and take over as though he had built it himself, as though sitting beside this fire was his due.

The major felt his hand gripping the trunk of an apple tree. It was unlike a Cherokee to feel this way. Property and place should belong to no one. One lived, took what was needed, thanked the Great Spirit for providing it, then died and was buried to become the earth once again. But his land was his. He had fought, built, dug, planted, harvested, and prayed on this land. It had his fingerprints all over it. How could he just sign a paper, get into his carriage, and ride west? He was not like Junaluska and those others in the mountains. Yes, they were Cherokee, too, but now different in some way. Could it be that he, himself, had changed? In their rush toward progress, had he and Ross lost what it was to be Cherokee?

As the sleeping forms on the ground stirred toward wakefulness, Ridge was reminded that he had not slept on anything other than a White man's bed since he had followed Andrew Jackson through the swamps and the tangle and the heat in Florida. His pockets held coins, not beads. He and his wife, Suzanna, rode in a carriage. The clothes he wore were sewn by tailors in Atlanta and Knoxville. He owned no moccasins and he and not chipped an arrowhead since his youth. The men who camped in the orchard now sat up and eyed him silently were Cherokee. They knew without asking why he was outside, touching one tree after another. They understood the need for goodbye. They still dreamed. Perhaps, they were more Cherokee than he was.

The old major made his way to the top of a rise and turned back to the east where he could see much of his farm. Sun was on the roof now. More fires were kindled and men were beginning to huddle in clusters around them. A little farther along the ridge, he came to a slab of granite protruding like a worn tooth from the ground. It was the "grinding rock." On one corner, there was a circular dent in the stone where women and, later, slaves ground corn. Laying his hand into the depression, Ridge wondered how many times a mortar had struck this spot to make such a deep mark.

Behind him, a sound in the frost-stiffened grass made him turn. It was his son, John. For what was perhaps the first time, the major looked at his son as a man, not a boy. He had always thought that he had seen John as a man, but clearly this was the first time. Why had he not noticed this before? Signs of middle age were there, in the eyes, in the jaw line. Even his hair that stood in a curl on top of his head as Suzanna's did was not as black as it had been in his youth. His stride, although upright, now seemed more measured as though he planned where best to take each step. John had become the politician that the major had always envisioned, a leader, a counselor, a molder of the course of the tribe. John, as the son, was everything that the major wished himself to be. He was smooth in a gathering, slightly understated in a way that made others want to agree with him. He had an instinct for consensus. The only time that he had displayed brashness was when he became fixated on the White girl who he eventually married. But the major understood that.

"This is a biblical moment, father," the son said as he settled onto a spot next to the elder Ridge on the grinding rock.

The father nodded, although he did not entirely understand the allusion. He had sent John to the Christian school when he was a boy because he knew that he and the tribe would benefit. It would make them less strange to the burgeoning population of Whites surrounded them. But he could not push himself to become Christian. The old ways were too deep within him. Harmony with place was worth more than everlasting life. Even if he went through baptism, he would still rely on old intuitions and—when they came again—dreams. He never regretted giving his son over to the missionaries; that was part of the way that their world was changing. And he liked many of the stories that John had brought home. Now, it was a comfort to liken himself to this Moses of the Old Testament, his role being to lead his people out of bondage in Georgia. And it was a story that was well received by the people who would follow him. But Ridge knew that no matter what face they put on this treaty that he and John were about to sign, there would be no peace with it in their lives.

From down the hill, the smell of cooking drifted up to them. Suzanna would be preparing the last of the hog that they slaughtered. There would be one last meal in this house—a feast of all that they could not carry west on the wagons—and then they would gather at New Echota and sign the paper.

Both men found it hard to talk now, each with his own sense of how they had arrived at this point. Both had seen it coming for almost two years, but as the moment of signing the document approached, the steps required to physically get themselves to the document in New Echota and sign it grew more and more difficult to take.

Just then, their silence was broken by the approach of running feet from behind. A young Cherokee raced toward them, hair flying behind him in the wind. As he came, he called breathlessly, "Major, Major!" The runner fell to the ground beside the rock, gasping. "They . . . they caught one."

"One what?"

"He . . . he was from Ross."

John stood. "Where? Where was he?"

The man pointed in the direction of New Echota, four miles away. "He was on the hill, overlooking the road. He was in a thicket with a rifle."

"Let us see this man," said the major, aware of how easily a sense of command came to him. They followed the runner back down a path that led to the road that led to the village that had served as the Cherokee capitol. As they walked, others who had been sleeping nearby saw them, and sensing a purpose to their march, joined in. Within a half mile, the party met another party coming toward them, Elias Boudinot in the lead. In the center of the group they held a young Cherokee, dressed like a woodlands dweller. "He came from a Middle Town clan," the major said to John. "Tennessee, perhaps North Carolina."

The captive was no more than twenty, but had the determined bearing of one on a mission. Although bound fast to a lateral pole across his back, the man showed no fear. His face had the high cheekbones of pure Cherokee and his eyes burned with anger. When he looked at the major and John, both sensed death in his face.

"What does he say?" asked John.

"Nothing. He has not spoken since he was captured," explained Boudinot.

"He is from Ross," put in the major, and just as he did, the captive turned his eyes toward him. Ridge knew that if the Creeks had men like this years ago at Horseshoe Bend, he would never have crossed the river alive.

"Let's kill him," said one in the crowd.

The major considered the idea, then shook his head. "Let us send him back to Ross. He will be Ross' witness to the treaty. But, first, make sure that he does not fire his rifle or any other for a long time."

The others looked at the major, then comprehending, led the young man to a rock where he was forced to sit. His right hand was placed on the surface and the butt of his own rifle was brought down hard on the back of it. Bones broke with a sound like the cracking of a stick. The man did not cry out, but gasped at the shock. The procedure was repeated with the left hand.

"Tie him to a tree," ordered the major. "We will eat. Then when we go to sign the treaty, this man will be our witness. Later, he can tell John Ross that the Cherokees now belong to Oklahoma."

Knoxville
Tennessee
June 23, 1836

Brevet General John E. Wool was beginning to understand how Solomon's baby must have felt. It was a story that he had heard many times in his father's sermons, one that his father liked retelling because it spoke, he said, of the human weakness of perpetual ambiguity. However, Wool suspected that his father would have liked that story less if he had to live it. In living it, he would have discovered that what passed down through the ages as wisdom could be seen by the actual participants as caprice and murder. That's how the general felt today, for there was no solution to the problem that faced him that would satisfy any one. The problem was his orders, his impossible orders. No matter how he carried them out, they would probably sink his career, a career that he had been building carefully and with the dignity imbued in him by his minister father.

Wool now walked the thinnest of tightropes that a military man ever had to walk. And, except for the fact that this accursed president so ordered it, the situation was not really a military problem. It was a civilian problem, if it was a problem at all. If the president wanted a large portion of this nation moved from one part to another, it was the job of federal marshals to carry out the task, not the Army. The Army was for settling international disputes and defending the shores, not getting involved with domestic messes. But here he was, John Wool, a newly promoted general officer in this steamy backwater trading post, and the first thing that he had to deal with was the Army, itself.

He was saddled with twice as many troops as had been expected. He had just arrived in the village of Knoxville after a hard journey on horseback from Washington, and now he had maybe a week to gather supplies for what he had been told would be a contingent of 1200 volunteers. Inexplicably, that number had doubled. Whose idiotic idea that was would probably never be known. Most of the unexpected arrivals were from Georgia, and overly eager to get their job done. The great number of men in his command only served to make his already odious task more conspicuous. He needed tents, he needed utensils, he needed food, he needed feed and hay for horses, he needed blankets, he needed ammunition. Somehow, these must be found in this backwater village and made ready for the men. It was an impossible task to accomplish in a month. But he and his staff of four officers had, at best, a week.

Bad as they were, logistics were only a small part of his nightmare. His orders said that he was to assess the situation in the Cherokee Nation and determine the Indians' willingness to be transported to what was to be their new home in Oklahoma Territory. But that was as far as clarity went. What was unspoken—the orders behind the orders—was what put him on a tightrope. The president had picked him personally for this task. And it was common knowledge throughout the War Department that the president wanted the Indians moved before his term ended, at the close of the year. But the nation was divided almost exactly down the middle on the Removal Act. And that included the War Department. There were those who did not want anything to do with the business of removal and did not want the army involved. It was a political thing. No professional soldier wanted to touch it. It had the smell of "career killer" all over it. The general who presided over this one could well be skunked.

Rising from an overstuffed chair in the boarding house where he had taken a room, Wool paused to stare vacantly out a window that was streaked with rain. His reflection showed faintly in the glass, a middle-aged soldier who, in spite of gradual softening of his body, still looked like a soldier. His hair was combed forward in the napoleonic style of the day, covering a hairline that marched to the rear with each passing year. His face was lean and his mouth turned down in a line that was slightly severe, perhaps a little judgmental. Piercing eyes befitted the office of Inspector General. Maybe he was not as dashing as Andrew Jackson in uniform, but it pleased him to think that those who saw him on horseback had no doubt that he was a general. It was a slight vanity, a sin that his father had not entirely scolded out of him, but today, that was about the only thing that pleased him.

Beyond the window, the western slope of the Smoky Mountains rose up, across the river from Knoxville. The tops of the mountains were obscured in clouds. The rain had not cooled the air, but had made it sultry, and he opened a gap in his tunic to try to get some relief. For a moment, he tucked his right hand inside, just below the second button. Yes, he did look like a general, perhaps a New England version of Napoleon. The thought pleased him more than it should, he knew. Vanity could get in the way of soldiering. Wool was committed to being a soldier, and had been conditionally raised to the rank of general officer because he was not given to rash or impulsive judgement. He understood War Department politics. After all, he had been in the Inspector General's chair, through multiple reorganizations and assignments of specialization and dithering of congress, for twenty-one years—longer than anyone else had. His was not a popular task, but he was good at it and did it efficiently, without brutality. Few complained and few sabers were broken. The thing that he regretted after all these years was that his career often seemed to be stalled. Infantry was how he had been trained, and he had risen rapidly there. But his last promotion was two decades past. True, he was a brevet general now, but his real rank and pay were that of a colonel and would stay that way unless he were confirmed. People—including the president—were watching him. What he did here in this little Appalachian trading post would have a lot to do with him keeping the star that he wore.

But the assignment here revolted him. There was something beyond the military or even political considerations of removal that bothered him. Perhaps it was the familiar voice of his father, buried deep in his breast, that told Wool that this was just plainly, obviously, overwhelmingly, immorally wrong. Unfolding the paper that was labeled "Special Orders of the War Department," he began to read them again. "You are ordered posthaste to the Cherokee Nation to assess the willingness of the Cherokee people . . . " to move from homes where they and their ancestors had lived since before the time of the Grecian Wars.

For six years, Wool had heard the arguments about expansion of the nation and making more room in the mountain region for the White settlers . . . about the agreement in 1802 between the State of Georgia and the then weak federal government to cede to Georgia a huge portion of the Cherokee Nation . . . how the only way that this could be accomplished was by moving the Cherokees to a distant place beyond the Mississippi. For Wool, these arguments simply added up to putting the Indians where they would be out of sight, out of mind—and out of the way.

The general pressed his fingers to the glass and sensed the dampness on the other side. He needed time to think his way out of the dilemma of his orders. The problem was, they were unethical and unkind, but legal—just barely. They were supported by the will of Congress, which had knuckled under the president by enacting the Removal Act of 1830, by a majority of a single vote cast by the Speaker of the House. Since then, the nation had alternately dreaded and rejoiced that the situation would come down to where Wool found himself today. Three of the other five "civilized tribes" had more or less acquiesced to this terrible law and had moved to Oklahoma Territory. The Seminoles had resisted with war and were in the process of being subdued. The Cherokees, on the other hand, had resisted with peace, confounding the government—and president—for six years. And they had almost won. Through two court challenges, they had gained the distinction of "sovereignty" from the pen of Chief Justice John Marshall. It had seemed, for a time, that the Cherokees had thwarted the greed of the Georgians and the vindictiveness of the president. But they had underestimated the enmity of their former ally. Andrew Jackson, man of the people, hero of New Orleans, the man who had won battles with the aid of the Cherokees when he, himself, was a general, had arrogantly and abruptly turned his back on the Cherokees and refused to obey the court and Marshall. As he inferred, in a contest between Andrew Jackson and John Marshall, it was Jackson who commanded the troops.

So, now the troops—2500 strong—would be coming to determine how to take the Cherokees from these old mountains to a land that was as alien to them as the backside of the moon. John Wool would play a part in this sorry action. He was good at organization and logistics. That's why they picked him. He would assess what needed to be done, assess the will of the Cherokees to continue resistance, and outline a course of action that would evict them from their homes. And, he would eliminate their ability to resist by taking their guns.

Orders. It all came down to orders, what to do about his orders. To remove these people would be despicable; not to remove them would be insubordinate. And it would probably cost him his star. It was Solomon's baby all over again.

Turning from the window, he paced slowly in a wide circle, hands held at his back. But first things first. He would need a miracle to find all the materiel required to bivouac 2500 men—in a week.

Valley River Camp
Cherokee Nation
July 29, 1836

John Wool not only hated to lie, but also he hated to tell less than the complete truth. It was the father-minister's influence again, he supposed. Nonetheless, the report that he was preparing was a work of art for what it did not say, and it sorely taxed his ability to verbally dance around the ideas that he wanted to say. After all, the report was to the Secretary of War, and how one said things at this level determined one's future in the army. So, instead of explaining the naked attempts by the local White settlers, including many of the militia now in his command, to steal and plunder what little the aboriginal people in these mountains had, he tried to stay with the barest of facts. The truth was, it was becoming apparent that it was Wool's hand alone that held back what would otherwise be a stampede by the local settlers to dispossess the Cherokees. But there was no way to put that into words without sounding inflammatory. The time was coming when the Indians would be forced to move; anyone could see that. But the settlers were restless and did not want to wait to grab what they could of the spoils. Already, Wool had angered many with his policy of strict even handedness between Whites and Indians. But he could not say that in the report because it was not what Washington wanted to hear. Washington wanted positive news that would reassure them that the Removal Act, passed six years before, was, in fact, going to be accomplished.

Pacing beside the river where he had made camp

after leaving Knoxville, Wool unfurled his orders and read them for what felt like the one-hundredth time. They required him to, in classically obscure War Department language, to ". . . ascertain the condition and probable designs of the Cherokees ."

Their condition ? He could choose to respond oafishly and say that, save for a few in the New Echota area, these people are subsistence farmers. They live in or near small villages, raise fundamental crops which include two types of corn, get what meat they eat from the forests and streams, have their own customs and language, do not take to grazing animals, and store food collectively to get through the winter. What Washington feared was that the Cherokees might be organized enough for war. They had fought removal through the courts and won. But when the government went ahead with it anyway, would they respond with force? Could Wool tell them that?

Their designs ? That was easy: To remain in these mountains where they had been for ten thousand years. Those few with whom he had talked had never heard of Oklahoma and knew nothing of it. They were a generally peaceful, if not passive, group, in some ways naive to a fault. But in other ways, they could be crafty, shrewd, and unpredictable. How a forced eviction would hit them he had only a vague idea, but it was not good.

So, it came down to this: Would they rebel if forced to leave? From his first impression of the Cherokees, Wool thought not, particularly if he disarmed them. That was one of his tasks here, to confiscate their guns.

So, how would he describe all that to the Secretary of War? For a moment Wool wanted to trust the man and tell him how disgusted he was with this assignment, and maybe even go farther and mention his contempt for a president who would turn a soldier into an evictor. But Wool knew that a relationship with superiors was not founded on trust. It was a soldier's quandary that one could trust another on a skirmish line to take a bullet that was meant for you and to die if necessary, but never trust another when it came to matters of rank. It was a lesson that Wool had learned as a cadet. The temptation for one to make mischief with the perception of another was irresistible. Inevitably, it compromised truth and lead to this Hamlet-like predicament in which the general now found himself.

He stopped pacing and watched the river. The water flowed slowly in this broad valley, not as it did in the higher mountains where it rushed and tumbled in a white spray. Here it was clear and a deep green color, reminding him of the rivers that he had seen in Western Virginia, the Rapidan, the Jackson, and the Cowpasture. He had chosen this spot for his headquarters because it gave access by river to the three states in which most of the Cherokee Nation lay. By heading upriver, his troops could travel into North Carolina via the Valley, Nantahala, Tuckasegee, and Little Tennessee rivers. In this region, travel along rivers was the only way soldiers could move about. Roads were few, and many of the mountains were too steep for horses. Some along the Nantahala were even too steep to climb on foot. Turning down stream, the Valley River flowed into the Hiawassee, no more than a half mile from his camp. That gave access to Georgia to the southeast and Tennessee to the west. The plan was to scout locations to set up stockades along these rivers, and farther west. Most of the émigrés—if they could be called that—would have to travel past this location. It was here that Wool could find out what he needed to know and make his reports.

In the sultry twilight, he was distracted as a fish rose to the surface, showing a golden stripe along its flank. It drew in an insect that hovered just above the water, then returned with a small splash. It was a magnificent creature, bold, clearly the master of this stretch of the river. Wool envied the fish, its purposefulness, its lack of entanglements. He sighed. He would write the report and say what he had to say, but only a little of what he wanted to say.

A little over two weeks earlier, the general had dispatched a company of men to scout the Indian nation and assess the intent of the Cherokees. Under the command of a Capt. Morrow, the company took a route along the rivers, as far as the Qualla settlement in North Carolina, then through Franklin and into Georgia where they stopped at most of the larger settlements, including what was left at New Echota after Georgia had forced the Indians to abandon it. Finally, they passed into Tennessee.

In Georgia, the principal resistance to removal ended the year before when a splinter group of Cherokees signed the Treaty of New Echota with the government, then left with two thousand of their followers for Oklahoma and the promise of land and reimbursement of $5 million. Reviled by the remaining seventeen thousand Cherokees, the Treaty Party, as they came to be known, traveled west under threats of death. Behind them, the political infrastructure of the Cherokees collapsed, leaving only one man as a leader: Principal Chief John Ross. He had assembled a new tribal headquarters in Red Clay, Tennessee. The soldiers would make that their last stop there before returning up the Ocoee River to camp on the Valley River.

At Wool's direction, they were to assume the guise of a survey party, and to remain strictly neutral in the growing agitation between White settlers and Indians. They were to gage feelings about the Removal Act, but keep their own opinions to themselves. They were to quietly survey the Cherokees to determine how many guns that they possessed and their willingness to give them up. And, they were to observe the populace, in general, to discover any trouble spots now, or any that were likely to develop in the future.

Morrow was the right man to lead such a mission. He had been a captain for a long time, and barring decimation of the officer corps, he would remain one. A cautious, plodding man, one would not notice him in a crowd, except for a shock of unruly brown hair that stuck out from under his hat. He always seemed to need a hair cut. With Morrow in command, the population might not remember that they had been visited, and all the men would come back intact.

Indeed, Morrow and his company had returned the night before. This morning, his face showing little sleep, he handed the general his report. It was well reasoned, detailed (even where necessarily vague), and troubling. It had a lot to say about the abrasiveness of Principal Chief John Ross, and his antipathy towards the departed Treaty Party that included some of his former friends, including a Cherokee by the name of Major Ridge who had fought with Andrew Jackson at Horseshoe Bend.

The report also included a geographic diary of their expedition. Wool thought it would be useful reading for those soldiers who would follow them after this mission was concluded, and made a mental note to have Morrow expand it as a separate document. It described ". . . a gorge along the Nantahala River as too steep to scale without ropes and pocked with natural caves where a few men or a family in need of shelter could stand. Vegetation was most dense here. The valley of the Tuckasegee River to the east is more passable, but some of it is flanked by steep, bald rocks that no horse could scale. Soldiers in transit would be limited to riding a trail along the river. On up stream, the Oconaluftee splits from the Tuckasegee and flows from deep in mountains where White men would find it almost impossible to traverse. Across a high pass, we descended into Macon County. Settlements are larger and valleys wider . . . rivers show more silting, supporting greater agrarian enterprise. In Georgia, our party crossed a steep gorge at Tallula . . . spectacular, but difficult. Mountains are reduced to rolling hills beyond this and transit is much improved. The party is able to average thirty-five miles per day. The trek out of Georgia and up toward Tennessee follows parallel ridges. At New Echota, we found evidence of considerable enterprise, now ceased. At Chattanooga, a river flows slowly in great sweeps. It looks navigable. East of Chattanooga, we crossed the Ocoee and made our way back toward North Carolina, along much white water. Hills grow steeper again, and loom up like a fortress before us. Travel is slow again ."

After allowing the captain a few more hours of sleep, the general spent the rest of the afternoon questioning him. Now, as Wool strolled by the river, he digested what he had learned. Morrow ". . . found no evidence of hostilities, but daily efforts of Whites to dispossess Indians of their land and houses. " That meant that the rumors were true. With so much waiting to be grabbed, the White settlers could not wait. There had been skirmishes already, shots fired from ambush, several Indians killed in Georgia, probably by settlers searching for gold. Further instances of unrest could not be allowed to happen. These people would never give up their guns if they believed that they would be raided at any moment.

The next day, Wool figuratively held his nose, signed the report, and posted it to the Secretary of War. He set most of his staff to work surveying the area around the camp for a suitable site on which to build a stockade. Much of the militia was directed to start felling trees that covered the slopes of the valley. They would need logs to make sheds for supplies, for corrals, and for guard towers. Eventually, the towers would become the corner fixtures of stockades, but for now they would serve to protect the camp and give the men something to do.

Then the general took two aides and an interpreter and rode up the river toward a settlement of Cherokees, located about fifteen miles from the camp. He needed first hand information about the attitude of these people, and to make sure that what he had reported to the Secretary of War about the Cherokees was true. The plan for his party was to present themselves at the homes of several Indian families and see if they would turn over their guns voluntarily. No attempt would be made to take them by force. If they did not hand them over, the party would simply leave.

They set an easy pace up the Valley River, following its slow sweeping turns. The morning was bright, almost cloudless. Summer's humidity had been replaced by drier air that hinted of fall that would begin to make its appearance in a month. It would be hot later in the day, but the soldiers would not be as uncomfortable in their tunics as they had been when they first arrived in Knoxville.

The general twisted in his saddle to glance at the

interpreter who accompanied him. He was a round little man whose proportions gave the impression of a berry resting on a plum. Dark hair was plastered tightly to a pale scalp. There was a cherubic, harmless quality about him. Wool tried not to be deceived. Appearance was a first cousin to vanity, and drawing conclusions from one's appearance could be foolhardy. The man, whose name was Will Thomas, had come from the Qualla region along the Oconaluftee to meet the army, to intercede, as he put it, between the soldiers and the Cherokees. He operated trading posts on Soco Creek and across the high country, and supplied both Indians and White settlers with seed, harnesses, plow points, cloth, nails, flour. Morrow's report had mentioned him, saying that he was buying parcels of land in the area, primarily from White settlers who had moved there in the 1820s. It said that he had a close affinity for the Cherokees. He was good with their language, a tongue that to the general sounded tortuous, and had demonstrated his skill with a few Cherokees who approached the camp. Still, the man was something of an enigma. If he were a proponent of the cause of the Cherokees, he did not say so overtly. In fact, he said very little, which Wool found odd since he expected one who was a proponent of a cause to be more loquacious, even evangelical. But not this round little man. He spoke little unless spoken to. Perhaps, he was aware of how unpopular his cause was and that he was surrounded by over two-thousand militiamen, all of whom could become land grabbing settlers as soon as they were mustered out of service. Wool concluded that it was a brave thing that Thomas did in showing up at the fort.

"Mr. Thomas, how should we show ourselves when we come to an Indian's home? Should you go ahead and tell them what we are about?"

The small man met the general's eyes. "No, sir. We should shout our approach from about a quarter of a mile away. It's the polite thing. Then go in slowly as a group, with weapons holstered."

Before noon, they spotted a cabin across the river on the north bank, and set out for it. Thomas went ahead of the soldiers, stood in his saddle as high as his short legs allowed, and let out a bellow. They plunged single file into the water and rode across in a shallow area where they could see the bottom. Climbing up the other bank, Thomas yelled again, breaking off in three dog-like yips.

"Is that much noise necessary?" the general asked amused.

"The courteous thing is to be sure that they know that we are coming in," the little man replied seriously.

As they drew closer to the cabin, the air was filled with the smell of wood smoke and something baking. The cabin, itself, appeared to be a one-room affair, resting among a stand of large balsam trees. In winter, sun would come in under the lower branches and warm the house; in summer, the trees provided a deep shade. The front of the house faced the river so that the occupants could watch any approach. A small, brown-skinned woman stood in a garden that spread with little attempt to organize it in front of the cabin. She could have been thirty-five or forty years old. Standing with a weed in one hand, she shaded her eyes with the other in a way that hid most of her face.

Thomas lead the riders to within easy hailing distance, halted, then said something in Cherokee. Without a reply, the woman turned and went into the cabin. After a moment, a man appeared. He looked slightly older than the woman, but not much larger. His hair was beginning to go gray, and he was dressed in a simple shirt and leggings. Aside from his nut brown skin, the only things that distinguished him from a White settler were the moccasins that he wore.

Thomas dismounted and motioned for the others to follow. They approached a large, flat rock to the right of the cabin and sat when the Indian settled there, cross-legged.

Thomas spoke a few words and the Cherokee made a brief response. "He says that his name is Red Wing." Thomas then introduced the general and made some preamble that the soldiers took to be a statement of purpose for their visit. At first, there was no reply, then the Indian made a long rambling comment which, judging by the expression on the interpreter, was unexpected. He turned to the general who was doing his best to maintain an air of dignity while seated on a rock, and said, "He asks . . . he asks why you bring . . . untruth to his house. He asks what is this lie that you bring."

Coming to disarm, Wool found himself disarmed. He had been exposed to great power and charisma from generals, to the oily craftiness of the Secretary of War, to the thundering bluster of the President. But with these, Wool had always been able to stand his ground. But no man had ever seen through him so quickly. For a moment, the effects of all the schooling, the marching, the parades, the formations, and the rank were lost. Whatever he had imagined these people to be he realized that he had vastly underestimated them. Suddenly, Wool felt naked on the rock. He was sure that the others could see.

"General?" an aide said, touching his arm.

"I'm fine," Wool snapped, sharper than he wished. Turning to Will Thomas, he went on. "Tell him that I will not lie to him."

Thomas translated that and received another rambling reply. "He says that you come in a cloak of lies, that you have some . . . business . . . some enterprise that you . . . misrepresent. He says that you come with many men to where the two rivers meet, yet you come here with only four. He wonders why you left so many behind. If he does not do what you want of him, will you bring all the rest another time?"

Wool would not liked to have played chess against this unschooled aborigine. He would have owned all Wool's pieces almost before they were placed on the board. And the odd thing about it was that he said all this without a trace of posturing or bluster. There was only the steady gaze of those soft brown eyes. The general had expected some hint of fear from the man, or at least apprehension, but not this complete absence of any concrete reaction. He simply did not know what to make of the man.

"Tell Mr. Wing that I represent the government, and the government has asked, in preparation of the great move to the West, if the Cherokees would relinquish their firearms."

Thomas turned and translated. At first, there was no response from the Cherokee. Then, he abruptly rose and disappeared into his cabin.

"General, what if he comes out shooting?" his adjutant whispered from behind.

"He won't," interrupted Will Thomas.

"How can you be sure?"

"He's seen your side arms. His wife is inside. He'll bring out whatever he has to protect her. Same as you would do if you were in his position."

Sure enough, a moment later, the Indian emerged from his cabin carrying a muzzle loading rifle, upside down. He came face to face with Wool and handed it to him with both hands. The general stood and accepted the rifle.

How many generals rode away from a skirmish, objective in hand, feeling thoroughly defeated? Wool had no stomach to go on and encounter more Cherokees. One was enough. On the ride back to camp, he thought about what he had learned, to see if anything useful could be passed on to his subordinates who would begin to sweep the Cherokee Nation in search of guns. As afternoon shadows lengthened from willows that clung to the riverbank, he called a halt and dismounted. Directing the men to fall out, Wool took a diary from his tunic and walked to the trunk of a large sycamore that had been uprooted and lay half in the water. He removed his hat and leaned against the trunk, and began to replay in his mind the encounter with Red Wing. He wanted to get down his impressions before they faded or became mixed with events at camp.

After a few minutes, his adjutant approached tentatively. Wool looked up from his writing. "Sir, we may have been handed a feather, not the chicken."

"What do you mean?"

The captain held out the rifle. "This piece hasn't been—couldn't have been—fired in twenty years. The trigger is rusted frozen. The hammer can't even be cocked."

Wool examined the muzzleloader, testing the trigger himself. It would not move. Peering into the bore, he found more rust. Along the stock were teeth marks where some rodent, probably a rat, had gnawed. He nodded, understanding the captain's allusion.

"If that man hunts anything—and they say that they all do—he doesn't do it with that rifle. He has another."

"So, Captain, to my notes describing these people as smart and tenacious, would you add the word 'devious?'"

Fort Butler
Cherokee Nation
September 7, 1836

John Wool reread the letter that lay in his lap and was tempted to crumble and toss it into the cook fire that smoked a few feet away. The letter was from the president, written from his home at The Hermitage, near Nashville. Wool could not tell whether Andrew Jackson was an egotist with a napoleonic complex or was simply drunk when he wrote the document. In any case, the words did nothing but increase his contempt for the man.

Jackson's instructions to him—could these really be construed as orders?—always had a way of being at variance with those that he received from the War Department, and pushed him toward action that compromised his integrity.

The guard on duty near his tent refused to look at the general. All the men knew better. By now, it was no secret what he thought of Andrew Jackson. Word like that gets around. So, when the news spread that a letter had arrived for the general from the president, both officers and enlisted men made themselves scarce. There were chores to be done outside the stockade that they were building—far outside.

The general did not notice their absence, focused as he was with maintaining self-control while words of gross insubordination screamed in his head. But that is where they must stay. He looked at the letter again. It ordered him to prevent the Principal Chief of the Cherokee Nation from "*. . . holding any council of his people for further discussion of the treaty of removal.*" In other words, he was to ride to the Cherokee council grounds in Red Clay, Tennessee, and gag John Ross.

In deference to his minister-father, the general almost never swore, but he swore now, silently. A vein in his head throbbed. It wasn't enough that Jackson had set him on a path to evict the Cherokees from their homeland, now he wanted him to silence them, too. He would be damned to hell if he would do it—or court marshaled if he didn't. Perhaps, it was the same thing.

First of all, Wool did not have the authority to silence Ross, orders or no orders. Even the president did not have the authority to silence Ross. In the time that he had been posted to the Cherokee Nation, he had learned that Ross was not Indian enough to be Indian. Therefore, if he were not Indian, then he was a U.S. citizen by right of birth. And Jackson could not silence U.S. citizens because it was unconstitutional. He sighed to relieve some pressure on his head. This was another perfect Jacksonian conundrum in which he found himself.

Looking up, the general was surprised to find the stockade grounds almost deserted. Not even his aide was there. "Trooper!" he shouted at the guard, "where is my aide?"

The single chevron on the guard's uniform flinched. "Outside the compound, sir! I . . . think."

"Get him. And tell him to bring his maps." Then as the soldier was scurrying away, he shouted after him. "And bring me a courier . . . with provisions for four days."

Angry as he was, Wool was not so angry that he would be impolite. He sat down at the writing table in his tent and dashed off a quick letter to the president: "*Per your instructions, sir, I am on my way to the council grounds of the Cherokees, in Red Clay, Tennessee.*

Respectfully yours, John Wool." It was terse. It committed him to nothing. It was good enough for who it was for.

As his aide approached, map case in hand, the general looked up. "Send a messenger to that fellow from the Oconaluftee who showed up here, the trader. What was his name? Thomas, Will Thomas. Tell him I want him to go with me to Red Clay and act as an interpreter." The young lieutenant snapped a salute, then turned and left.

Later, when the riders had been dispatched, one to Tennessee and one to the Oconaluftee, the general turned his attention to the maps, still in a foul mood. Even the smell of the heifer roasting over a nearby fire was not enough to dispel his gloom. The journey from Fort Butler at the confluence of the Valley and Hiawassee Rivers to Red Clay would take three days, perhaps four if the weather turned foul. Red Clay lay in Tennessee, just north of the Georgia state line, and was the site of the Cherokee council meetings since Major Ridge's splinter group from New Echota had signed their treaty. The treaty, along with local ordinances restricting assembly by the Cherokees, had enabled the Georgians to run the Indian politicians—particularly John Ross—out of their state. As an act of defiance, the Cherokees had chosen Red Clay as their new council grounds because it lay just inside Tennessee, within sight of Georgia territory.

But a journey anywhere of any length was a chore for the general. What no one knew was that this man of dignity and bearing did not like horses and was convinced that they did not like him. In the years since he could ride, he had been bitten, bucked, scraped off on a tree, low-limbed, stomped, and rolled on. He had come to mistrust the beasts and could not understand why his fellow officers spoke of their mounts in terms that they usually reserved for warriors. The general was more comfortable at his desk, but that was a secret that he hoped to take to his grave.

With maps unfurled, he followed the Hiawassee River out of North Carolina, as it looped around mountains and made its way into Tennessee. Along the way, they would cross over to the Ocoee River and intercept the road there that would lead them all the way to Red Clay. When he had first arrived here in June and began to build Fort Butler, the general had learned not to attempt a straight-line passage through the mountains. This place was not like Ohio or Pennsylvania or Maryland or New York. There were places where horses—and most humans—could not pass. Thickets of laurel, vines, and briars lay like collars of tight, green fleece at high elevations. So, following the rivers, albeit longer, at least assured one of getting to one's destination.

When the interpreter Thomas arrived, he was briefed by the general, himself, and agreed to go with the soldiers. The general remembered that the man had kept to himself before, aloof from the soldiers. Now, he was more so, to the point of being edgy. He acted like a man with a secret, and Wool wondered if he could be trusted. After supper, the two sat in front of the general's tent and watched the fire die. The nights were getting colder and a blanket would be welcome later. In the morning, they would leave for Red Clay, but that would give Thomas a night to rest from his ride from the Oconaluftee.

"Mr. Thomas, what do you think we will encounter when we arrive at the council grounds?" The question hung stiffly in the air between them and Wool realized that he had been too blunt. Perhaps, he betrayed his own anxiousness. In any case, it was obvious from the other man's expression that a verbal frontal assault did not work with these mountain people.

Thomas removed his hat and scratched his head. "Resistance."

Wool perked up. "Armed resistance?"

"No, no. Nothing like that. Ross is determined to avoid a blood bath. But . . . for whatever reason you are going there, they know that it is not in their interest."

"I go there by order of the president. He wants no more debate about the question of removal."

"Do you mean to prevent the council from meeting?"

The general shifted uncomfortably. The man was, after all, a lawyer. He knew how to ask questions. "I am empowered to do so, if I see fit."

"Well, general, there you have it. You can't imagine that John Ross is not aware of that possibility. He is a lot of things, but he is not naive."

Almost against his will, the soldier felt a growing admiration for the civilian. He liked his orderliness, the precision of his words. The man showed none of the irritating disorganization that was common to his ilk. Wool sensed that he could deal with him.

The journey to Red Clay took them the better part of three days, and they arrived on September 13. The weather was good and the trees on the mountain tops were beginning to change color, poplar to yellow, maple to red. Had he not been uncertain about what faced them at Red Clay, John Wool might have been caught up by the gaiety of the season. But he rode on steadily through the rolling countryside of the lower mountains of Tennessee, his somber mood infecting the detachment of troops that rode with him.

Red Clay was not a new settlement or even a recreation of an ancient Cherokee village. It had been created out of the woods, to be a meeting place, and proved to be nothing more than a collection of sleeping huts that was dotted around a pavilion shelter, itself just a roof that rested on bare poles. A thatching of broom sage kept sun and rain off those gathered underneath. To one side lay a ring of stones, blackened by fire that had been allowed to die back to just a flicker. Although unimpressive, the place had an air of simple dignity and reflection. Several Cherokee men in colorful shirts of cotton and traditional headscarves greeted them respectfully, indicating a stand of pine trees where the men could tie their horses. No arms of any sort were visible, so the general issued the order to dismount.

Among the Indians gathering, there was no sign of John Ross. For a moment, Wool wondered if he would snub him by simply refusing to appear. After all, as Will Thomas had pointed out, Wool's mission to Red Clay was contrary to any interests of the Cherokees. But the mood of those who continued to come out of the woods and into the clearing of the council grounds was one of curiosity, not suspicion or hostility. They came and stood easily, arms hanging to their sides, with no hint of deception or aggression. It was clear that they were simply curious.

The crowd grew slowly, seemingly out of nowhere. When, perhaps, fifty had collected, one appeared among them who was out of place. He had the face of a Scot and the clothes of a merchant, black frock coat and white shirt and collar. He wore his clothes comfortably, and although he was clearly different from the Indians, they took no notice of it. But unlike his Indian companions, his eyes never left the face of the general. Wool was being measured.

The knot of men that included the White man stopped before the general, and stood silently. Then, after a long pause, the White man spoke. "I am John Ross, Principal Chief of the Cherokee Nation. Welcome to our council, general."

Wool drew himself to attention and saluted, as befitting a head of state. "I bear greetings from the president, Mr. Ross."

"I am sure that you do," Ross replied on a guarded note. "And how is General Jackson these days?"

"I am told that he is not well, but I have not seen the president since I left Washington in the summer." Who was this man, John Ross, and why did Andrew Jackson despise him? Clearly, the message behind the message in Jackson's letter spoke of rage and resentment. Since Wool had first come to the mountains, he heard rumors of bad blood between them. At trading posts, grunts and smiles passed when their names were mentioned together, as though some secret were known, but could not be publicly acknowledged. The general would have to remember to ask Will Thomas if he knew anything about that. If anyone would, Thomas would.

John Ross took a step backward and waved to split-log benches that lay around the fire ring. "General, sit with me and let us talk."

Ross was like a magnet and the general understood immediately why Andrew Jackson would not like him. Like two strange cats, the men probably could not coexist in the same room. Each needed dominance; and although each would use different means to get it, dominance was still the goal. (The fact that Jackson and Ross were natural enemies and that Wool felt nothing but contempt for Jackson did not make Wool any more comfortable with this little man who wore his welcoming smile like a mask.) But what Ross could not hide was the sense that he wanted something and whatever he wanted was the most important thing in the world to him. Wool knew other such men. They were usually politicians, sometimes ministers, or sometimes soldiers. He realized that Ross had just engaged him in a mental poker game. The stakes were high, particularly for him and his career. They were probably high for Ross, too, but he did not know that for sure. Now, they faced each other, two men with opposite goals. Wool had been sent here as a lever to pry John Ross and upwards of 17,000 Cherokees out of these mountains. John Ross, as everyone knew, was determined to dig in and stay put. How much he was willing to risk to accomplish this, no one knew. Would the Cherokees rebel? Outwardly, Ross spoke of peace and of not taking up arms. Certainly the people surrounding the general and the soldiers were peaceful. But how far would Ross go? Wool was not a gifted gambler, believing in order more than chance. He was a transparent man; that is probably why Jackson had selected him for this mission so that he could be read as events unfolded. These cards would have to be played very carefully. If there were to be aces had, was John Ross already holding them?

As the two leaders talked, soldiers and Indians mixed in the crowd around them, no longer mindful of a need to be wary of each other. They stood in respectful silence, warmed by the late afternoon sun. The general and the Cherokee leader seated themselves side by side on a rough bench, half facing each other as though they were two diplomats in a drawing room. The interpreter, Thomas, edged in and took a seat behind them. Perhaps, he was not necessary as Ross spoke English as well as the general, but it gave the soldier comfort to have him there, in case there was an aside spoken by Ross in the Cherokee tongue. Each man understood the value of representing the role that they played, and proceeded slowly into the conversation, like two boxers feeling each other out.

"This is a beautiful place that you have made here," the general observed.

Ross nodded in agreement. "It is a gracious land. I love my whole nation, but I confess that I love this rolling land the most." Sitting forward slightly, he asked, "Do you know my friend, Chief Junaluska?"

The general thought for a moment. "No, I do not know him."

"He lives in the high mountains, in a place called the Snowbirds. As the crow flies, it is not far from where your soldiers are camped on the Hiawassee. It is cold there much of the year. I am not sure that I could live there. It is a beautiful place, but I doubt that I could live there."

Knowing no other way, the general plunged into the reason for his mission, like a player betting heavily on the first cards dealt him. "Mr. Ross, I have come here because President Jackson worries that you and your people have . . . not accepted the terms of removal."

The merriment that had been in Ross' eyes vanished, and his face took on the look of someone who has seen danger. "We cannot accept what we cannot accept," he said evenly.

"You know, sir, why my troops are camped in North Carolina. Surely, you know and understand our mission."

Ross rocked back on the bench and glanced behind them, at Will Thomas. "We know every tree that you cut for your stockade."

Wool was surprised by these words, but did not doubt them. He made a mental note to double the guard when they returned. "I have to ask you, sir, what are your plans for this council here?"

"We plan to talk, general. We plan to talk about . . . options."

"Forgive my bluntness, Mr. Ross, but do any of these options include armed resistance?"

Ross smiled tightly. "In this case, general, your 'bluntness,' as you call it, serves you well. But to answer your question, no, we plan no armed resistance. How could we? We are few compared to your many. And, besides, I was under the impression that, in the region where your troops are camped, you are confiscating the arms of my people."

Perversely, the general felt himself relax. "If you are as well informed as you appear to be, sir, you know that the weapons that we have taken from your people are of the most pitiful sort. Mr. Thomas, here, can tell you that."

The admission let the tension out of the air between the men. Ross glanced to Thomas, and when his eyes returned to the soldier, the twinkle that had been there earlier was back. "We Cherokee are a resourceful people, General Wool."

John Wool had come to the moment that he had anticipated since the letter from the president arrived—no, since he had been first directed to the Cherokee Nation in June. He was at that ethical fork in the road, one path leading in the direction of strict obedience to the presidential will, the other in the direction of what his conscience told him was the right thing to do. The letter had specifically directed him to prevent this council meeting. But it was an unconstitutional order. It was the order of a king, not a president. To acquiesce was to join. To take the second path was insubordination. The president would be furious. Wool could almost see the man pounding the wall with his cane and cursing.

"Chief Ross, would you accept me as an observer to your council?" The unflappable Ross was visibly rattled. This was a possibility that he had obviously not considered. At worst, he expected to be told to disband; at best, he expected to be dictated the terms under which the council would be allowed to be held. But, by according Ross chief-of-state status, Wool put him in the position of playing the role of host. The general had hit on the one option that would confound them all: The president would not get the council disbanded. Wool may have hung his own career on a meat hook; that remained to be seen. But John Ross—as host to the general—could not explore the polemics of the removal issue that he had hoped to explore without being an obviously bad host in front of his own people.

The air seemed to go out of Ross. "General, you are most welcome."

Days later, as he rode back east along the Ocoee River, headed for his camp in North Carolina, the general smiled to himself. Perhaps he was not such a poor poker player after all.

Soco Creek
North Carolina
November, 1836

illiam Holland Thomas sat in a rocker on the front porch of his store and stared out at the clear, cold creek that flowed past. He knew with absolute conviction that it had been created by God, Himself, just for him, to watch, to contemplate, to remember. He felt no blush or sacrilege at this presumed link to divinity. It just was. He knew everything that there was to know about Soco Creek, where it started high in the mountains and where it ended, where it held fish, and the color it turned after a heavy rain. He knew where it fell over rocks with so much noise that one could not hear another person speak. He knew the springs that fed it and which ones produced the salamanders that tempted fish. He knew how the taste of it changed as one moved upstream. The whole length of Soco Creek was home to him as no other place had ever been.

`But for the first time since he had come here as a twelve-year-old boy with his mother from Waynesville, he thought of leaving. This was a bad time to live in the Cherokee Nation. Business was bad, the worst that he had ever seen, and there was no hint that things would ever get better. The Indians of the Oconaluftee region to whom he sold bits of cloth and nails and powder and seeds and buttons were now just sitting in their cabins, doing nothing. No one in these parts had planted a substantial crop in the last several years. They were just waiting, barely managing to hang on. The removal business had them acting paralyzed. They did not even hold their celebrations, and that had everyone unsettled, including the few White settlers who lived nearby. Thomas had no Indian blood in his veins, but he had lived here long enough to sense the rhythm of the seasons. In April, the fields were burned and the dirt was turned; in May the planting was done and fish put into the hills of corn to make it grow; in the hot days of summer, men fished and the women kept weeds from the garden; with the first turn of leaves, there would be harvest and the Green Corn festival; as the leaves fell, the men would hunt and trap and store the corn to dry in cribs; when winter was on, they gathered wood and lived life mostly inside, sleeping in the low "sleeping huts," around a fire. Thomas knew it all, felt it in his head. He knew when to stock flour and cloth and needles. He knew when to be ready to buy a hog, and how much a new knife was worth. He knew where five bee trees could be located and where the little garlic grew that flavored stews in late April. He knew how to skin a deer and where to take the tendons that make strong string. He was almost as much Indian as any of the people who came into his store. They knew and trusted him as completely as they could any White man. Yongaguska—Drowning Bear—of the Qualla Band had adopted him as a son; they even gave him a Cherokee name, Wil Usdi. Now he felt their confusion about the possibility of being removed to Oklahoma, felt it almost in his bones. But what he did not know was what was going to happen to them, or to himself, if they left.

It looked like they were going to leave. There was an army general in the nation now. He was building forts and trying to talk the Cherokees out of their guns. Will had gone to meet him, John Wool was his name. At first, Will had not liked him much. He came across stiff, like a dandy who had found himself in rough country. But the more Will was with him, the more he liked him. There was a basic decency in the man. It showed in the way his tone of voice said that he loathed his assignment there in the nation. And another thing, he was decent to the Cherokees whom he met. He may not know how to talk to them; he may not know what the three sisters are. But in the time that Will spent with the general, he never saw him treat an Indian badly. That said something, plus the fact that he had firmly instructed the militiamen in the company not to be aggressive with them.

Still, Will was depressed. It wasn't the first time. He knew the signs. Sometimes, this black mood seemed like his oldest companion. But today, the source of his depression was clearer than it usually was.

He would like to blame the whole fiasco on the group that John Ross liked to call the "Traitors of New Echota," the Ridges and the Watie brothers. It was their Treaty of New Echota that broke the logjam on removal of the Cherokees. But in more rational moments, he knew that they had simply reacted to their sense of being surrounded and politically out-gunned.

Perhaps, Will thought, he should just go back to Waynesville and practice law. He was young enough. It was boring, but he could make a go of it. Or, to hell with it, he would just do like that old fellow up on the Nantahala did and build a fish trap and live off that. But he didn't like fish that much. Something was going to have to change, and the change was going to be drastic.

On the far bank of the creek, Will Thomas spotted a figure moving. The person wore a tall hat with a brim that flopped down past his ears, as though the hat had been rolled and spent the night in a bag. Only Jonas Jenkins would wear a hat like that. Thomas had known Jenkins since the lanky man had come to these parts fifteen years before, from Virginia with his wife, Juliet. Jenkins was an odd fellow—but not bad in any way that Thomas could say. There was no hint that he drank too much or that he drove his animals too hard. On the contrary, he was unfailingly gentle and mostly social. If a taste of corn liquor were offered, he would take one, but had no need to drain the jar. He was, however, peculiar. There was an air about him of not quite being there. His eyes wandered in little jerks, like the flight of a damselfly, here, there, never quite coming to rest on any one thing. What he said was equally rambling. And, when one finished a conversation with him, you were never quite sure that Jenkins understood to what you had agreed.

For these reasons, Thomas had learned years before to keep conversations with Jonas Jenkins to what he termed "lower case thoughts," those that involved rain for crops, the height of corn, and the size of squash. He stayed away from notions such as politics, the rampant evangelism that was sweeping the mountains, and Indian affairs. Both men seemed to understand where the other stood on the Indian issue; that they both lived among them and were friendly to them was statement enough.

This morning, when Jonas reached the porch of Thomas' store, his eyes were wide with anxiety. Then, he uncharacteristically blurted out what was on his mind. "I came to ask ye, what's going to happen to 'em, Mr. Will."

Thomas did not respond immediately. Eventually, though, he managed a reply. "The Cherokees?"

"They're sittin' around like a rabbit surrounded

by hounds. They ain't hunting and they ain't planting, and they haven't since a year or two, at least nothing steady."

This confirmed what Thomas thought. The Indians throughout the Qualla region—although somewhat shielded by their special status as North Carolina citizens—were not immune to the pall cast over the rest of the Cherokee Nation by the threat of removal to the west. Kinship and tradition crossed all boundaries. Removal was like a pestilence, something that slipped up on them collectively just when they thought that they were safe. They had celebrated their victory in the Supreme Court too early. The game was clearly not over. Now, it was anybody's guess where this thing would go. And that is what Will conveyed to Jonas.

"But Mr. Will, these people been here longer than dirt. How can runnin' 'em out be right? I, myself, traded with 'em. I bought my land, fair and square. I didn't just come in and grab it like. Where's the right in that?"

"There ain't many like you, Jonas. Most folks don't care much what happens to the Cherokees."

Jonas spit and let it fall off the porch where he stood. It was another of his habits that annoyed Thomas, but he let it pass. "Don't know what to say about that. They been good to me. They gave me seed when I first came here, helped my wife some, too. You know, she was never strong. When we had extra of somethin', we'd give them some. That's how it was. They were just people like us, tryin' to get by."

In the years that followed, Will Thomas would not know from where his next thought came. But it would forever alter the course of his life. And, even as he spoke, he did not know how the idea would form or where it would take him. "Jonas, Jonas, if I asked you, would you sell me your land?"

Jenkins blinked. He had not expected this and did not see the point of it. "Why do you need my land, Mr. Will? You thinkin' about farming yourself?"

Thomas whistled, still trying to untangle where his thoughts were going. "No, no, Jonas. If all this removal business comes to pass, it's my guess that it can't be done without a big pile of federal money being turned over. All the talk I've heard says that there will be reparations paid to the Cherokees, in some way, some form. What if . . . now stay with me on this one . . . what if somebody could use that money and buy them some land, say, here in North Carolina?"

The reply came faster than Will expected. "Kinda sounds like using government money to buy back land that the Indians already own."

"Yeah, that's one way of looking at it."

Jonas took a deep breath, then spit again. "Sounds a mite tricky."

"Would be. Everything would have to be done on the sly, by someone acting for the Indians. The government would stop it in a minute if they knew what was going on beforehand. Once it was done, though, it'd be done."

Jonas rocked back on his heels, studying the idea. He was opposed to chicanery on general principles, but if chicanery was needed to fight chicanery, then maybe it would not be so bad. "You need my land for this, huh?"

"I just said it, Jonas. Your land, my land, a person would have to start somewhere. You've got that nice spread up the creek. It was a part of that tract that was opened up for Whites back in '19. Maybe it could be a seed to build a wider tract."

"I'd need a new place, but that's not impossible, I reckon."

"No, there are some nice coves on down the Oconaluftee and Tuckasegee. Ground looks good. Wouldn't be too hard to plow. Room for some stock to graze. Good water. Good home sites. Pretty much what you have now, but not so steep. Could be even easier to work."

"Where are you goin' with this, Mr. Will?"

Thomas shook his head, uncomfortable with the underdeveloped idea. "Wish I knew. This notion is not whole. I just see a kind of preserve or reservation forming up around the Oconaluftee Cherokees. Some of them are already considered to be citizens of North Carolina. Maybe that's something to build on."

"Do you reckon that would put an end to this removal business?"

Thomas signed. "Probably not. I hear tell that there are places in the world where the ground cracks open every now and then, and everything shifts around after that. Sometimes there's fire and smoke that comes up out of the cracks. They say that nothing is ever the way it was before. I think, Jonas, that the earth is about to crack open here."

Snowbird Mountains
Cherokee Nation
March 3, 1838

The snow was heavy as Tsali moved along the bank of the stream in the high country known as Snowbird. He had just come through a pass on the westerly end of a great valley. At the time of creation, the Great Buzzard that formed the mountains and valleys must have struck this ground with a mighty blow to part the land because the valley that lay before him was almost farther than he could see. The going was slow as the snow came up to his ankles. He had been here before, as a younger man, and always the wind had been blowing as it does high in the mountains. But for the moment, the air was dead still and smelled of the cold sweetness of snow. Later in the morning, it would pick up again, but as he walked now, he could hear every sound, including his footsteps.

He moved deliberately like an animal born to this place, hesitating, shifting deftly to the next solid footing, then pausing to sample the air. A White man would have walked steadily in one direction or another without innate caution. Another Indian watching such a person would know the difference. Certainly, Euchella would know the difference. This morning, above all others, Tsali wanted to be Indian. He walked in search of this friend of his sons, and the son of his friend, the boy from Soco with whom he had hunted in his earlier years and spoken around many camp fires.

Somewhere in this great oblong bowl of a valley, Euchella would be watching. He had been in Snowbird for almost three months, ever since word had come that more government troops were coming and that they would sweep away the Qualla Cherokees just as they would sweep away the rest of the Cherokee Nation. Euchella had reasoned that if they could not find him, that they would not take his wife and daughter. It had seemed like sound reasoning to Tsali when he heard it. Soldiers would not make this war on women. Even Euchella's wife agreed that he should go. But in this instance, Euchella did not get a chance to prove or disprove the strategy with the soldiers because, in his absence, his wife and daughter died of starvation.

Tsali had seen starvation in the Cherokee Nation only a few times in his sixty years, and always at the end of a hard winter. It was rare because this was a land of plenty, winters tended to be short, and his people were instinctively generous. They would not ordinarily let a neighbor starve. But this was a winter like no other. With the influx of soldiers beginning two summers before, word spread throughout the Cherokee Nation that all the people were being taken away to some far place in the west. Soldiers were building something called stockades in Georgia and Tennessee, and now in North Carolina, too. It was said that they would put the Cherokees there first, penned like cows, then move them on large boats on a great river that Tsali had never seen. Already, they had sent troops out to gather up the guns of the Cherokees. The leaders of the Cherokee Nation had fled the capital of New Echota, but from Ross Landing in Tennessee they urged no resistance to the soldiers. "We will fight this thing the White man's way, through the courts," they had said. And they won, for a brief time. There had been much rejoicing in the nation. Runners had been sent out with the talking leaves that said that the people could stay. But then a peculiar thing happened; the government paid no attention to its own judges. The soldiers came anyway. And behind them came White men who wanted their land and their houses and their things. These men had not been allowed to take them yet, but unlike the Cherokee, they could not hide what was in their hearts. Tsali knew that it would come to that.

He had heard all of this, in his cabin on the Nantahala, and had begun to have a recurring dream, about a mad dog and a soldier who wept. The dog attacked his master, and later the soldier rode out of the hills with tears in his eyes. Along with everything else, the dream made no sense. This was a time like no other to the Cherokees.

Not knowing what would happen to them, Tsali and his wife had neglected their own garden. They had little corn, and the squash and beans that they had planted were overgrown by weeds. By fall, their corncrib was not full as it should be. No one in the nation had even celebrated the Green Corn Festival. Tsali marveled at this, their most important festival, forgotten. A nation-wide malaise settled on the Cherokees. Food grew scarce. Men were afraid to hunt with their rifles because that would be an acknowledgement to the soldiers that they owned one, which they were loathe to do. As the corn ran out, Tsali resorted to working his fish traps on the Nantahala, but the water was so cold that his legs would grow stiff and he would have to abandon the water after only a few minutes. If he had no fish in that short time, he and his wife slept hungry.

About the time the corn ran out, Euchella left for the Snowbird. Tsali knew that Euchella had not left thoughtlessly, that he had supposed that his family would be cared for by the others who lived in the Qualla settlement. But what he had not counted on was the Cherokees' reluctance to ask for help. This was particularly true in the case of Euchella's wife. It was, after all, her sacrifice that made his resistance possible. Should she prove weak, he would have to abandon his hideout and come home. She resolved not to let her hunger—and that of their daughter—become his weakness. So, she and her daughter ate what they could gather and made thin broth from grasses and mushrooms and stalks that had dried in the garden. The child endured stomach cramps with little complaint, but by January, she had lost her childhood plumpness. On the rare occasion when neighbors appeared with food, the wife met them at the door and, in a very un-Cherokee fashion, accepted their offering and sent them away brusquely. Her manner fooled no one; in fact, the people of Qualla spoke with pride of her sacrifice. But it did give her neighbors an excuse not to come around often. Then, one day near the end of February, a neighbor came bearing a small pouch of corn meal. She found the house quiet. Two bodies lay huddled together near a fire that had long since grown cold.

So, now in April, Tsali walked like a Cherokee along the narrow river in the valley of the Snowbird. It was his fourth day of traveling from his cabin on the Nantahala. He did not want to think about how he would tell Euchella the news about his family. Perhaps, Euchella already knew. Tsali wished that he did.

The morning grew very bright and sunlight sparkled in the snow that had fallen during the night. Tsali looked in wonderment; the sight of it was still as overpowering as it had been when he was a boy. He could not leave this land. He must find a way to remain. For a moment, he forgot the cold against his legs and the hunger that now never went entirely away. His eyes swept the terrain in front of him, looking for tracks or anything that was out of place, but there were only the parallel dots in the snow made by a foraging rabbit. He moved on.

As he walked, Tsali questioned his wisdom for looking for Euchella here. Snowbird was a big territory, with many laurel thickets where a man could hide. Why had he chosen this valley? He had simply come here out of instinct. Why? Then it became clear: It was because Tsali would have come here himself to hide. From any location on the slope, one had an unobstructed view of a half mile up and down the valley. And there was cover on the slopes where a man, if he were still, could not be seen. And on the opposite side of the north slope, there was a thicket so dense that dogs could almost not get through. If a man were discovered, he could retreat across the rim of the valley into the thicket. That was as safe as one could be if one were hiding out here.

Tsali took his time and did not go directly to the spot where he figured Euchella to be watching. He would approach in the Indian way, meandering, indirectly. Along the southeast slope of the valley, he stopped and remained still for a long time. The air smelled of the fresh snow that had fallen during the night; there was no trace of smoke. The old Indian concluded that if Euchella were making a fire, he did it at night, and probably in a cave or depression where it could not be seen. Overhead, two squirrels emerged from their nests in a hickory tree, and came down to search for nuts that they had hidden in the fall. Barking at each other irritably, they broke the dead silent dawn in the valley. Tsali searched the landscape again. Rabbit tracks appeared again, in a meandering trail near the stream, then disappeared into clumps of broom sage. Probably, that was how Euchella fed himself, on the squirrels and rabbits here. He looked for a snare, but found none. If Euchella were here, he was careful, very careful.

Just as he was about to move on, Tsali caught sight of an outcropping of granite. On a bare spot below an overhanging spruce, the stone lay gray against the surrounding whiteness. On top of the slab sparkled small shards of something black and shiny. It was obsidian. Euchella had been making arrowheads. He was hunting in the old, silent way, as he had learned as a boy, before everyone had the guns that made hunting easy, but noisy. He had left behind the chips removed from the points. Perhaps, he assumed that a White man would not see them for what they were. Perhaps, he assumed that another Indian would.

Tsali climbed high on the slope. His knees ached from the cold. In a year or two, the pursuit of the seasons would overtake him, and he would not be able to do this. He hoped that he was good for one more hunt before he had to have meat brought to him by kindly neighbors. No man wanted to become that old. Maybe the coming of the soldiers had changed all that. Their presence lay in the valleys of the Cherokee Nation like a pestilent fog. John Ross had said that the Cherokees would stay here. But still the soldiers built the forts, it was said, to hold the people before they were taken to the west. The confusion that it caused was terrible. It had made the people talk in fearful speculations when they should have been working and hunting. It had made them forget

Euchella's wife and daughter.

Circling on the eastern end of the valley, Tsali moved carefully toward a small knot of laurel that grew on the turn to the northern flank. An instinct came to him, as uncertain as the soft beating wings of an approaching moth. It told him that Euchella was in there. Tsali had long ago learned to trust these impulses on a hunt and moved toward the thicket. But even in the brilliant sunlight, he was unable to see into the tangle of limbs. Then a voice came from within the thicket, as though it could talk, stopping him in his tracks.

"You are a bad spirit old man. I could have killed you ten times, though you walk like an Indian."

Tsali moved closer and looked into the hideout. Euchella had made a nest in the thicket like what a rabbit would have gathered. Weeds, leaves, and broom sage were clustered in a mound with a hollow center. There was no evidence of fire so this was only a lookout point, a spot from which he could watch both prey and predator. As though he read his thoughts, Euchella offered, "I sleep in a cave within the great thicket across the ridge."

"You have learned something on all those hunts," said the old man.

Euchella rose from a squatting position within the thicket. His lean features had become gaunt, and he had the look of a hunted man who sensed that he was almost trapped. "A few nights ago, I saw a figure—a man—in a dream. He had no face, but his body was covered with ashes. Today, when I saw you, I knew that it was you in the dream. The notion was not good. I watched you since you came into the valley. Your search was deliberate, so I knew that you were not hunting anything but me. Why do you hunt for me, old man?"

"I bring you bad news of your family. They did not survive the winter." He said it, not obliquely in the Cherokee way, but bluntly. Too late, he realized the hurt in his words. Perhaps it was the times that made him abandon his manners.

Euchella did not flinch or make a sound. He stood as though the frigid air had frozen him in place. A breeze swept up the valley and shook the limbs of the trees above them. Somewhere, two squeaked together, making a sound like an old iron hinge.

"How did they die?" the younger man asked quickly, a tone in his voice like the sound of bark being stripped from a branch.

"The village ran out of corn. The people had nothing to share."

"When did you learn of this?"

"A runner came to my cabin five days ago. They thought that I would know where to find you."

Euchella sat back down abruptly. This was more than he could comprehend. The implications of their deaths touched him, touched his neighbors—even touched the soldiers who had invaded their lands. It was the thing that he had feared most and yet dared not think possible in his one-man rebellion. Now, harmony and balance were lost, and that required retribution, from the person or the family that did the harm. That was the law, the law of the ages, the only law he knew. But who was at fault? Was it the whole Qualla village that had, in their confusion and fear, failed to tend their crops in the summer? Was it the soldiers who harassed them and came to their cabins to take away their guns and spread the paralysis of fear? Was it Euchella, himself, who had put his protest above their safety? It was too much.

He could not see the truth. But if he could not resolve this, then the spirits of his wife and daughter would wander, lost forever. The dog inside him howled in grief and frustration.

Tsali watched his friend in pain, and thought of his own wife. The love that a man felt for his woman was not a thing that men ever truly spoke of. The games, the teasing, the cooking, the arguments, even the bedding—these things could be said. But the feeling behind them was too fierce and consuming and terrible to be acknowledged. As young boys, they learned to never admit to fear, so the awful beast of this love went unnamed. Yet, as they became men, those who felt it knew it was akin to the pure, uncompromised passion that the boy felt for a girl when he was a youth. He learned to mask the feeling, but the quality of it never changed. The heart of a man who loved his woman was still the heart of a boy. The greatest problem was that they do not know how to give it up when it is lost.

"If I would have understood that you were the man in my dream," Euchella said finally, "I would have come back. But I did not understand. I am a warrior, not a shaman."

Tsali nodded. With little fanfare, he withdrew a small pouch from a bundle that he carried. "No one in the nation celebrated the Green Corn Festival this year. You and I must not forget the tradition." He offered the pouch to Euchella who looked inside and poured out a handful of cornmeal. "Corn is still our life. We must not forget, even if it is just you and just me." Slowly, they chewed the dry meal until it was gone.

Soco Creek
North Carolina
April 1, 1838

Euchella did not like following the path of a White man, even one made by his old friend from childhood, Jonas Jenkins. Because of settlers like Jenkins, uncertainty gripped the Principal People. All that they were—their traditions, customs, legends, language, stories, and now their land—was compromised by White men. Even their dreams had been invaded. But here he was, in Jonas' old house, warming himself in front of a fireplace that Jonas had built when he had come here in 1821. Outside, dawn was turning the blue blackness of night to blue gray. He had slept only briefly since his arrival the night before from the Snowbirds. When he had gone there, he had thought that his flight was the defiant gesture of a warrior. A Cherokee could still be independent and live the way that they lived before White settlers arrived. But the only ones who noticed were his own people, and, in the end, they did not count because it did not serve to bring others to stand against this disintegration that was happening to the Principal People. Only, now, his wife and daughter were dead, and the soldiers were said to be coming next month to move everyone away.

Euchella had returned to Soco accompanied by Tsali, but when he entered his own cabin farther up the creek, he realized immediately that he could not stay there. The spirits of his wife and child were there and he could not remain near them. They crept around the single room and were in the things that they had touched—the pots, the baskets, the quilts—

when they were alive. They had died while he was away, starved and alone. As Euchella sensed the restlessness of their spirits, he knew that he must somehow settle the wrong that had befallen them or else they would wander forever. It was the Blood Code of his people. Harmony, he had to restore harmony, and to do so, his wife and child must be avenged. So, he left his own house and had gone to Jonas' old house which now stood empty because Jonas had moved his family down to another farm on the Oconaluftee.

The morning fire crackled as Euchella considered these things. How could he avenge their deaths when he did not know whom to strike? White men brought this about. Perhaps, he should pick two out and kill them ceremoniously, but which two would be the right two? He did not know the answer to that. Maybe it made no difference. Maybe any two White people would do. He could wait beside a trail that led to the trading post of Will Thomas. White people came to that place every day. He could kill two of them as they passed.

Somehow, the thought left him unsatisfied. There was no ceremony in killing men from ambush. That was murder, and would just bring more trouble. Nothing would be settled. Men would come to hunt him and he would be a fugitive for real this time. Likely, they would harm other Cherokees as they had done in Tennessee during the years of his youth, in retaliation for raids back then by the Cherokees. No, these deaths must be clearly symbolic, their purpose obvious. Only that way would harmony be restored to Soco Creek.

As he watched the dawn grow lighter, Euchella remembered a song for the dead, and sang it to himself and thought of the spirits of his wife and child. Could they know that he sang the song for them? Would they hear it?

Rain began to fall with a measured tat-tat-tat in the leaves around the house. It would rain most of the day. He was glad for a place to be out of the weather. The snow and wind had been brutal in the Snowbirds. Although he had been taught how to build a nest like a rabbit, there had been times there when he thought that he would never be warm again. He shook constantly, except when he had willed himself not to. Now, however, he could sit here before the fire in Jonas' house and decide what to do. He could think about how to satisfy the Cherokee code and take retribution for the loss of his wife and child. Or . . . he could see their deaths in some other light. But, he did not, at the moment, understand what that would be. Could he just do nothing? Under the threat of removal, the entire Cherokee way of life was crumbling like an old fallen log. In his escape to the Snowbirds, he had hoped to strengthen the resolve of the people to stay, to act like warriors, to fight and die like Cherokees, if it came to that. But their resolve had failed. They had been worn down by a generation of bad news. Land had been lost in successive bites. The leaders of the clique in New Echota had sold out the majority of the tribe and fled west. The Principal Chief, John Ross, had been evicted from his own home in Georgia and made to live in Tennessee. And now it was said that soldiers were coming, not just the few who were already in the nation, but a whole army of them. Perhaps, they might not take the Cherokees from the Oconaluftee region because some were citizens of North Carolina and therefore exempt from removal. But who knew with soldiers? No promises by White chiefs had ever been kept. So, this whole valley where he had grown from boyhood to manhood had become as lifeless as a grave. Everyone had given up and stayed huddled in their cabins. Only he, Euchella, seemed willing to fight, but he was no longer sure that fighting was the right thing to do. He sighed. He had been right before. He was no shaman and it would help to have one now to help him work out this puzzle.

Later, after he made a patty of corn meal and browned it on a smooth hearth stone, he ate slowly and thought about what to do. The spirits of his wife and daughter wept as they wandered aimlessly around his own cabin upstream. Their tears were in the rain. He could feel their presence, just as he could sense the approach of a fox or a deer when he was hunting. They were trapped in the valley of this creek, unable to continue the journey to their spirit home. Only two avenging deaths would restore harmony to the Principal People and unlock the gate that held them here.

Without understanding why, Euchella pushed off the rock where he sat, grabbed his bow and began to walk down the creek. He moved cautiously, not wanting to be seen. By the time that the sun was well up in the morning, he could see smoke rising from the chimney in Will Thomas' trading post. At this point, he climbed off the trail and slipped along the mountainside until he had covered a wide arc around the settlement. No dogs barked or birds scattered to alert the people inside the post of his presence. Below him, he could see the trail along the creek through the new sprouted leaves. Euchella settled into a thicket of rhododendron to wait and watch who went by.

Hours passed as he saw a few clusters of people come and go. Then later, two men, whom he did not recognize, walked separately to the trading post, then returned, heading west again, bent under the weight of sacks of meal. They wore the drab colors and floppy hats favored by White settlers. He watched them walk, resting their loads now and again. Each time they stopped, he could have put an arrow into their backs. Notching one onto his bowstring, he sighted down the shaft. It would be an easy shot. He had the advantages of surprise and elevation. His arrow would lose little speed as it sailed downward. At this distance, he could probably put it through the spines of each man. Neither would know what hit him. There would be little noise and death would be swift.

Euchella looked to the sky, then listened for the heartbeat of the earth for signs, but there was nothing. No cloud, no cry of a bird . . . nothing. All he could hear was the faint babble of Soco Creek, so he eased back the tension on the bow string and watched as each man disappeared down the trail to the west.

Noon settled into afternoon and the day grew warmer. Sunlight brightened the trail and sparkled off the flowing water of the creek. For the first time that year, Euchella saw a dragonfly. It flew in a darting, broken path along the edge of the stream. The earth was coming to life again; he could smell it in the damp soil beneath him. But this renewal gave him no comfort because he was perplexed. Why could he not kill the two White farmers? Each had been a perfect opportunity. He could envision their bodies lying in the new grass beside the creek, and the outrage that would follow. He would have to leave again, himself, but that was not a great problem. He was accustomed to living off what he could find. He could go back to the Snowbirds, or to the thickets high on Alarka or Deep Creek. A man could live in these places for a long time, undiscovered. The code of the Principal People did not require that the executioner know the person to be sacrificed, just that it be done to restore balance for the initial loss. But, why did he hesitate?

Unable to answer his own questions, Euchella resolved to wait, to meditate some more. Somewhere there must be an answer. So, he picked up his bow and returned to the house of Jonas Jenkins.

When night settled, he ate the last of the stew, then climbed the hill behind the house to a huge rock projecting over the valley that he remembered from childhood treks. As a boy, he had watched Jonas from this spot as he went about his farming chores. Jonas had shown an almost Indian-like reverence for place and kindness toward his animals. This puzzled Euchella because his father had cautioned that not all Whites were like that, that he should be wary of them.

Clouds drifted off and the night sky turned deep. Euchella felt something, a presence, behind him. A predator was moving cautiously. It was in a tree, over his right shoulder, probably an owl. The hunter in the man sensed the anticipation of the hunter in the bird, and knew what would come next. A great commotion arose in the tree and leaves and twigs showered down. For some moments, the attack continued, but in the darkness, Euchella could not tell if the squirrel whose nest was assaulted had escaped or had been caught by the owl. Whatever the outcome, it was the order of things. If the owl won, it would feed and its life would continue. If the squirrel escaped, it would build another nest that would probably be attacked by another owl on another night. In any case, the balance in the ancient struggle of hunt-and-escape held. And balance brought order and peace.

Euchella's gaze fell to the roof of Jonas' cabin. It

sat there like the squirrel's nest, a flimsy haven in the face of a predator. The chill that he felt at that moment came from inside him, not from the night air. There had been much discussion within the Cherokee Nation of Junaluska's dream of an owl attacking a squirrel's nest, and how that had been a sign of the treachery of John Ridge and the other tribal leaders in New Echota. Now the owl was back. Was this another sign? Was the owl telling Euchella to avenge the deaths of his wife and child by killing Jonas Jenkins?

That night he sat cross-legged in front of the fire. He had found a fallen locust near the cabin, and the burning limbs put puffs of pungent smoke into the room as they popped and showered sparks out of the fireplace and onto the dirt floor. The great fireplace was the only thing that Euchella envied about the White settlers. For a cabin so small, this one was enormous. When he was building it, Jonas had painstakingly collected flat pieces of granite from along the stream. Then he had located a thick vein of yellow clay in a nearby hillside, and used that for mortar. More clay was spread over the inside burning surface to act as fire clay and protect the granite which was known to crack or even explode if it got too hot. Finally, Jonas had mounted a piece of walnut log as a mantel, and oiled it until it was almost black. The opening in the fireplace was so large that if he stooped his shoulders, Euchella could stand in it. This kept the cabin warm as Jonas and his wife slept along the far wall. This was a good thing. Euchella had grown up sleeping in a sleeping hut where everyone lay around a fire in the center and smoke drifted out a hole in the ceiling, only sometimes it did not drift out so well and people would cough in the night. He had built one for himself and his wife. But this fireplace was better, the way it sucked smoke upward and sent heat out into the room.

As sparks flew out, he realized that it did not matter if one fell into the straw bedding and set the cabin on fire. This, he decided, would be his last night here. Tomorrow, he would do what he had to do, and then maybe he would never be able to come back. In the light of the fire, the killing of Jonas and his wife now seemed inevitable; all signs pointed to it. And as soon as they were dead, the spirits of Euchella's wife and child would be free to go on their journey.

For the first time since Tsali appeared at his hideout in the Snowbirds, Euchella slept an untroubled sleep. When he awoke at dawn, he tested his bow and the points that he had fastened into the sourwood shafts of his arrows. Everything was ready. Outside, the misting rain had returned and would mask his travel to the Jenkins farm.

Euchella rose and deliberately ate nothing. It was better for a warrior to be hungry; he would move faster and think more like a fox if he were hungry. It would take a good part of the day for him to walk down the creek to where it joined the Oconaluftee, and then the remaining distance to Jenkins' new farm. Loading his pack, he quietly shut the door and set off. It would be a good day for revenge.

The lanky Cherokee moved like a cat along the trail beside Soco Creek, feet touching lightly on the rocks that littered his way. The ground was soaked from the rain and spongy so that when he walked on it his moccasins left impressions in the humus that filled slowly with water. To prevent anyone from detecting him later, Euchella would leave the trail near Jonas' cabin and make his way through the brush. By the time anyone came looking for him, the rain would have settled the leaves where he walked. The rain would also keep the White settlers who lived nearby indoors; he knew from experience that they did not like to be out in damp, soaking rains. And, the Cherokees would be indoors, too, because that is about all that they did these days. He could walk the whole distance unseen. It was, indeed, a good day for a killing.

When he reached the confluence of the two streams, the darker water of Soco Creek discolored the green flow of the Oconaluftee. Euchella stood on the bank and wondered if this would be the last time that he would lay eyes on this place. He shrugged off the thought. He had no time for that. Fate would bring whatever it brought. For all he knew, he could be hung a week from now for what he was going to do. Deliberately, he raised himself up on a rock above the river, then plunged off into the woods. It was slow going this way. A mountain and a couple of lesser ridges lay between him and the Jenkins farm.

At the top of the first ridge, Euchella paused and looked back again over the river below. A fishing eagle soared overhead with its eyes also on the water. In the mist, it cast no shadow. That, too, was a good sign. Like the eagle, he would leave no tracks to be followed.

Later in the day, when Euchella came down the mountain and emerged from the mist, he could see the Jenkins farmhouse where it stood at a point where the valley narrowed. A corral and shed for stock lay against the hillside, below an outcropping of rock. The place showed its newness and Jonas' penchant for meticulous construction. The logs of the cabin had been squared with an axe, then cut on their ends to form perfect corners. They were not yet weathered and gleamed of new cut wood. There was also a window, so that they could see out the front without having to open the door, and a chimney rose up the back of the cabin. He supposed that the fireplace inside was much the same as the one in the cabin on Soco, except that, for mortar, this one used the red clay that was more common to the region. Poles for the animal shed and gates were poplar, skinned of their bark. Against the hillside stood a small spring house made of stone.

Euchella retreated to a cluster of muscadine vines above the stock pen to wait for Jonas Jenkins and to consider how he would die.

As he had done the day before, Euchella tested his bow string and found that, in spite of the rain that would soften the dried gut and the wood, it was taut enough to send his arrow across the animal pen if necessary. He would strike Jonas here, then go inside and kill the woman with his knife.

But something troubled him deeply about his plan. In spite of the signs being in his favor, Euchella felt a great darkness inside. When he was a boy, Jonas had befriended him and had let him load and shoot his muzzle-loading rifle. He remembered the moment that he had delivered his mother's gift of the life-sustaining seeds of beans, squash, and corn. There had been meals of fried fish and stewed squirrel taken with Jonas and Juliet in their cabin, before the great fireplace. In a sense, Jonas' well being had been in Euchella's heart. He had to remind himself that his true heart, his Cherokee heart, belonged to his wife and child. He must put them first and avenge them. The law and customs of the Principal People were clear.

When Jonas emerged from his cabin, stooped and wearing his hat that was too big for him, Euchella tensed. His hand clutched the bow, holding an arrow in place on the string. Long ago, he had learned that if one sat perfectly still in the woodlands that you could be almost invisible.

The farmer moved through the slop of the pen and pulled feed from the loft of the shed that stood to the side of the hill. Two cows, a goat, and his old horse moved in close, gathering in an impatient circle to be fed. Jonas spoke to each as though they were children. The goat, however, would not be stilled and between balling cries, it tried to butt its way past the others.

As Jonas bent over to grab the animal by its horns, his sight was averted from the hillside. Euchella raised his bow and drew back the string. The arrow would strike him at the base of his neck. It was a perfect shot, no more than thirty yards, with a twenty-foot trop. He had killed a bear with just such a shot.

But his hands would not move, as though they were locked. The bow string began to cut into the two fingers of his right hand. After another moment or two, his left arm began to tremble slightly from holding the bow.

Below him, the farmer seemed to be talking to his goat, and, impossibly, the goat calmed down as though it understood the words being spoken. Kindness seemed to flow from the man like mist descending a mountain. As the animal ceased to struggle, Jonas fed it from his hand.

Euchella relaxed his grip on the bowstring and watched the scene below. Rain dripped from the leaves and onto his face, but he ignored it. As the goat continued to feed, a quietness spread across the valley, and it seemed to Euchella that the world, itself, had stopped and was collectively waiting for him to decide what he would do. This was the moment of the true sign. As he drew back against the bowstring again, there was a heaviness in his hands as if the bow and arrow had turned into some unknown metal of great weight. He knew at that moment that killing Jonas Jenkins would be a bad thing, it would be murder, and not vengeance. Killing the woman would be even worse. All this became clear now.

The Blood Code . . . what would he do about the code of the Principal People? How would he explain his failure to the spirits of his wife and daughter? Where would they go? Would they forever be trapped in the confines of Soco Creek? Could he find some other way to bring harmony to them?

Like an itch in his head that could not be scratched, Euchella hated questions and the uncertainty that went with them.

Puzzled and defeated, he stood and hung his bow over his shoulder. At that instant, Jonas Jenkins sensed motion in the woods above him and stood also. The two men stared at each other for a long moment. When he had lived on his farm on Soco and Euchella had been a boy, Jenkins had known him to watch from the woods, probably curious about the ways of a White man. But this was different. From the look on the face of the Cherokee, he sensed that some enormous moment had come and gone. A feeling of relief that he could not explain swept over him.

Then, just as abruptly as he had seen him, the Indian disappeared into the woods without a word.

Franklin
North Carolina
May 30, 1838

In his short time in the army, Jonas Jenkins, learned to ride hard, look busy, and to keep his mouth firmly shut because he knew that he was soldiering for the wrong side. One could not fault the logic that put him into Company F of the North Carolina Militia. Becoming a soldier would get this business of removing the Cherokees over with as fast and painlessly as possible. It was going to be done, no matter what. He would get the few dollars handed out for enlisting. That would help buy stock for his new farm. And, keeping his mouth shut would keep him from getting his head cracked open by a fellow militiaman who believed in the removal of the Cherokees with all the conviction felt by those who guard an unfair advantage. There were a lot of them in this group. Jonas figured that if they did not know how he felt—that he really wished that the Cherokees could stay—then, chances were, they would leave him alone. He just hoped that they did not learn that he had sold his original farm to Will Thomas. That would be bad. Folks were beginning to catch on to what Thomas was up to, buying land for his "reservation."

Many of the men with him were a sullen, frustrated bunch, particularly the few who came up from little towns just across the Georgia border to join his outfit. The land of the Cherokee Nation that would soon be theirs could not be theirs soon enough, and they hated Indians the way that they hated snakes. Removal was the next best thing to extermination—which, Jonas suspected—they would have preferred.

Each day, they hoped that their service would turn into a fight. They needed a fight, perhaps to justify what they were doing. That's all they talked about at night, around the campfire.

In the face of this, Jonas spent as much of his time in the saddle as possible. Mealtimes were difficult. Words, cruel words, were said that were hard for him to hear. Jonas mostly did not respond or just shrugged when something mean was said. As it was, his silence was beginning to cultivate an entirely new group of people who thought him peculiar.

The weather had not helped the attitude of the soldiers, either. Sometime early in May the rains that came with almost daily frequency stopped. This pattern was replaced by a high, hot sun that left the air dangerously dry. What corn that was in the ground became stunted. The nearby Cullasaja River was a foot below its normal level, and dropping. On the mountainsides, the trees quickly lost the vibrant colors of spring and took on a withered look. Insect swarms followed the men wherever they rode, and even those who normally did not smoke kept a cigar lit just to keep gnats away from their eyes. At night, the men laid green limbs on the cook fires to keep a heavy layer of smoke in the camp.

The heat and bugs and then the dust put the militiamen in a foul mood, raising their aggression as they went about their work. Fights broke out over whose turn it was to gather wood and where a man might place his bedroll.

On this morning, the area commander—a militia captain by the name of Thomas Angel—directed that a platoon of men reconnoiter the section northwest of Franklin known as Burning Town. Indians were said to be living in the region, near a waterfall. If found, they were to be rounded up and marched to Fort Lindsey, way down the Little Tennessee River, and interned there.

Jonas did not know how many men were in a platoon, but there were more riders with him than he had fingers. One fellow, whose name was Jones, rode near him. Jones was always near him, it seemed. He was at his right shoulder when they stood in their civilian version of a military formation. What Jonas did not know was that Jones was there because his name was next to Jenkins in alphabetical order. But Jonas did not understand that because not only could he not count, he could not read, either. He just thought that Jones was always following him and he was determined to ignore the man.

Overnight, dew had been light and as the men rode out in the early dawn, dust rose around their horses. The smell of human sweat and horse sweat trailed behind the column. Horse flies sensed it and followed in swarms, causing the men to swat wildly at the air. Jones was there, right behind Jonas, cursing and waving his hat at insects that seemed to take a chunk of skin every time they bit. Jonas would have been amused, but he was too busy keeping the flies off the back of his head and ears. There was much cursing as they rode. A regular army sergeant in a blue jacket led the column and tried to ignore the flies, but Jonas could see him flinch as he was bitten. Talk was that dog days do not come until August, when gardens are withered and heat lays in the valleys, sucking out even the walk-around energy of the people. But this year, dog days had come early.

The men rode along the broad, shallow flow of the Little Tennessee River, now and then driving their mounts into the shallows to get some relief from the flies and heat. The horses roiled silt on the river's edge, but the men did not care if the water that splashed them was muddy; they cared only that it was wet.

By mid-morning, they crossed the river and rode southwest, up a dark shaded creek. The sergeant issued a "no talking" order as they rode single file along a shallow gorge. Honeysuckle and muscadine vines were tangled in the trees above. Sometimes a snake would slide off the vines and into the water, startling a man or his horse. This drew a hiss from the sergeant for silence.

Jonas laughed to himself. The people whom they hunted already knew of their approach. In his experience, Indians were rarely surprised by visitors, and a column of soldiers, riding with serious intent, would be a thing of great curiosity to them. Perhaps, they were watched as they rode now. Eyes might be hidden within clumps of laurel, peering out. As they passed, a birdcall was whistled along. When Jonas listened, he could hear the same call as the column made its way up the stream.

The splash of falling water was heard for the last quarter of a mile that the men rode. The sound grew louder as they pressed upstream, until they hauled into a clearing to see a small waterfall pouring into a broad pool that spread out for about fifty feet from the base of the waterfall.

The sergeant halted the column. Ahead stood the strangest thing that Jonas had ever seen. A group of more than two dozen Indians stood at the edge of the pool. They were obviously aware of the soldiers' presence, but none looked in their direction. They just stared into the pool below the waterfall, transfixed. Even the seven or eight children among them did not move. No one spoke and there was no sound but the splash of water. The Indians just stood there, assembled for whatever was to come, staring into the passing stream with an absent gaze.

The riders froze at the sight before them, as though they had blundered onto a sacred rite and in doing so stood, themselves, in danger of damnation. Eventually, the sergeant had the presence of mind to dismount, and the others followed apprehensively. That it was a kind of funeral that they were witnessing, only Jonas understood. It was not a scene that he had anticipated, but now that he saw it, he was not surprised by it.

An elderly man in the group of Cherokees stooped to pick up a wrapped bundle that lay on the ground and began moving wordlessly toward the soldiers. The others followed. As they approached, the soldiers gave ground until they engulfed the cluster of Indians. Remounting, the sergeant rode to the head of the group and led them back down the way that they had come.

All the way down the river to Fort Lindsey, the soldiers rode with no word or even sign of recognition from the captives.

Jonas would never forget that day, and as the summer rolled on, it would be repeated over and over, in little settlements named Iotla, Cowee, Cullasaja. Whenever the soldiers arrived, the people were expecting them. On several occasions, they were not ready to travel or they sought to take more than the militia would allow, and this gave some of the militiamen the excuse to use the righteous force that dwelled like a bear within them. But even when they were pushed, shoved, and occasionally butted with rifles, the Cherokees did not resist. They went peacefully to the stockades because, way off somewhere in Tennessee, their chief, John Ross had sent word for them not to resist. Jonas would forever marvel at the degree to which they followed these instructions. In his short stint in the army, there would be no single act of resistance on the part of the Cherokees.

Qualla Region
Cherokee Nation
October 31, 1838

Second Lieutenant Andrew Jackson Smith liked his job, for the most part. Posted with General Scott to the Tennessee Valley to round up the Cherokees for transport to Oklahoma, he knew that it was the only avenue available for advancement in the army. With no big war in sight, this little domestic exercise—and his fortuitous name—was the only thing that would keep him from remaining a second lieutenant for the foreseeable future. If he could handle his assignments smartly and showed a little, but not too much, initiative, he might make captain by the time they all reached Oklahoma. All he had to do was avoid falling out of his saddle, literally, and looking like an over eager pup. Project a little reserve, a little self control, he reminded himself. When it was done, two bars would look good on his shoulder, and there would be a campaign ribbon to go with them.

The only thing that got Lieutenant Smith down was this damned Smoky Mountain weather. It started out hot and disastrously dry during the summer, so dry that the level of the rivers had been too low to transport one group of captives to the west. Many had died in the stockades in North Georgia and Tennessee, just from the heat. Then, as though to make up for the lack of rain, Mother Nature sent it with determination. For days on end, low clouds settled on the mountains and leaked their condensate. A break would come, then that would be followed by another week of rain.

At first, the soldiers of the 1st Dragoons welcomed the relief. Their tunics were no longer wet with their own sweat. Men could march for more than a couple of miles without fainting. But as the ground beneath their tents grew damp, no amount of trenching could keep out the water when the ground was saturated. Bedding became damp. Boots and saddles became damp, and eventually turned green. Firearms developed patches of rust. Someone had to constantly tend the fires in the camp because they could not be restarted in the morning with wet kindling. The trails that they rode in search of holdout Indians turned to mire. Horses skidded unexpectedly and riders fell. Smith knew of two young officers who had broken legs when their mounts went down. They would not be around to make their captaincy in Oklahoma. As September became October, the rain turned cold. Smith donned his greatcoat and it grew heavy and smelled of wool that was wet too long. Everywhere everything was sodden. Men on foot did not so much walk as they tossed their boots that were perpetually caked with mud. The mood of the soldiers turned sullen.

On the last day of October, Lieutenant Smith led a mixed group of regular infantry, mounted volunteers, and a single civilian, the trader Will Thomas, from Ft. Lindsey at Almond to the Little Tennessee River. Thomas was along to act as interpreter, if necessary. He had lived among the Cherokees and they trusted him. Including Smith, there were fourteen in his party. Their mission was to collect 15 holdout Cherokees that had been rounded up and held by militia near the confluence of the Little Tennessee and the Nantahala rivers. Almost all the other Cherokees had already been sent ahead, and this group was some of the estimated 300 who stubbornly remained. When they had taken charge of the Indians in the morning, Smith and his party headed back down river. The weather had broken for the day, but gave no hint that the rain would hold off for long. Glancing up as he rode along, Smith saw smutty clouds tucked between white ones, giving the appearance of a storm that was biding its time, gathering strength for another assault.

Smith watched the party of Indians and thought it odd how these few remaining holdouts behaved. If they could, they would slink away at the approach of soldiers and disappear into the trees without disturbing a leaf, invisible as a fawn. Then there was no finding them. To catch them, Smith learned that one had to keep them in sight. On the other hand, when they were surrounded, all sense of rebellion seemed to go out of them, and they would offer no resistance to being marched to the stockades.

So it was with this mixed party of Cherokees that Smith and his squad of men herded down the river toward Ft. Lindsey. There were men, women, and children in the group; some as old as fifty, he guessed; some as young as three. They made their way along the steep bank of the river, walking almost soundlessly on moccasin covered feet. No words passed between them, as though they understood how strange they were to these soldiers and feared that a single word might reveal their sense of displacement. But their eyes told it well enough. The bundles that they carried were the only possessions that they would take with them to Oklahoma. All in all, he decided, they looked defeated, almost funereal.

How the Indians felt about the removal was their problem, Smith had concluded when he first arrived in these mountains in the spring, with General Scott. He had a job to do. He could not afford to get caught up in the emotionalism of a people who were completely alien to him. Besides, most of the Whites around here did not think that they were quite human. Smith was not going to get embroiled in the rightness or wrongness of the eviction. It was a political thing. He'd heard the gossip about General Wool, and that was not the way he wanted to go. The president (and namesake, Andy Jackson) had said that this was what must be done, and that was good enough for Lieutenant A. J. Smith. After all, he had his captaincy to think about.

A rider approaching from far behind pulled him away from his thoughts. The man was a volunteer and was trying to get their attention by shouting and waving his hat. Smith called a halt and they waited for him to approach. It did not take long as the man was going as close to a gallop as he could along the rocky river bank. Pulling to a halt, he snapped the militia's version of a salute to Smith and shouted breathlessly, "There's another bunch of Indians up 'Lufty!"

Smith assumed that he meant the Oconaluftee River. "How many?"

"I seen eight. Hear tell there's nearly twenty, though."

Smith shook his head, irritated with the militia's imprecision. "Well, is it eight or twenty?"

"I seen only eight. That's what we've got captured. But they say there are more close by."

"How far away is the bunch you've rounded up?"

The man pointed up the direction of the Tuckasegee River. "Up past where the Lufty runs into the Tuckasegee. Maybe twelve, fifteen miles."

He could reach them by nightfall, Smith calculated. He would take the interpreter Will Thomas and three of his regulars—Perry, Martin, and Getty—and head up river to take charge of them. The rest here he put in charge of his sergeant and told them to continue on in the direction of the stockade. As he wheeled his mount and headed back to the mouth of the Tuckasegee, the others moved off behind him, as silent as they had been before.

Smith and his smaller squad of men made better time without the burden of captives. The militia rider came with them until the split in the river, then continued on his way up the Little Tennessee. Smith surmised that he would continue on until he reached the Nantahala. The militiaman had said that this new group of Cherokees was from the Nantahala area, and that meant that new farms were available for plunder. That was what the militia was for, he supposed.

By late afternoon, they passed a cluster of cabins at a place that was marked as Big Bear Campground on his map. Eyes from doorways watched them pass. It was a poor area, not much for farming as the ground was soft and had the smell of a swamp. All along the river, sycamores and willows clung to the bank, a sure sign of perpetual dampness. Above the settlement, they crossed another small river, called Deep Creek, that was noticeably colder than the larger, cloudier Tuckasegee. In another hour, they were in a wide meadow that lay just below the point where the Oconaluftee joined the Tuckasegee. That was one of the few places in the deep mountains where Smith had seen land that was worth farming. The ground, although soft, appeared to be built up with silt from the river.

Tilting back in his saddle, the lieutenant called out to the portly civilian who rode with them, "Mr. Thomas, isn't your trading post near here?"

A small man with a round face came alongside. "'Bout four, five miles from here."

"You know this country well. What's this up here?" The lieutenant pointed to an odd hill of dirt that rose up a little more than head high in front of them, almost in the middle of the otherwise flat field.

Thomas leaned forward to get closer. His face had a serious look and his reply was a whisper. "It's a burial mound."

Smith pulled his horse aside, unwilling to cross it.

"It has that affect on you, doesn't it?" observed the little man.

The other soldiers behind Smith followed and the party rode by the mound in a semi-circular path, relieved when they had it behind them. In another hour, they passed the confluence of the two rivers and followed the smaller one eastward. The going was particularly hard here as a tangle of laurel and rhododendron grew along the river and several times they had to cross back and forth just to pass. Then the valley widened again and they saw the smoke of a campfire.

The captives were settled around the fire. Except for one young male, they appeared not to notice the approach of the soldiers, but stared intently into the fire. Four members of the militia wearing various ideas of uniforms were arranged behind them, standing guard. One of the Indians, a woman who Smith guessed was at least sixty, stirred the embers next to a flat rock on which she browned a patty of corn mush.

Smith dismounted and returned the salute of one of the militiamen. "Everything OK here?"

The other man who wore a heavy coat and floppy hat cut his eyes toward the Indians. "We found 'em headin' up river. From what I can make out, they walked all the way here from Nantahala. Don't know why they were here."

Smith pondered the information. It was well over twenty miles to the settlement along the Nantahala River. The county called Haywood covered much of the region of the Cherokee Nation that lay in North Carolina. This group was either trying to reach the eastern part of the county where some Indians lived as free citizens of North Carolina, or else they had been trying to make the deep cover that lay along the Oconaluftee River. Already, the so-called Lufty Band of Cherokees—said to number between forty and one hundred—were hiding out where no White man could find them. It was possible that this bunch was trying to link up with them.

Smith studied them individually. Aside from the old woman and the young boy, there were three young men, probably under thirty-five, a woman about the same age, and an old man. Perhaps he was the old woman's husband. All sat with frozen expressions. Smith could read nothing of their mood from them, save resignation.

Near a stand of pines at the edge of the field, he and his men hitched their horses in a picket line. One soldier, a private named Perry, was assigned to see to them and feed them. He had been a little too aggressive toward the earlier party of captives—he called them "nits" and liked to brush up a little too close to them with his horse—so Smith thought to keep him away from this group as long as practical. The civilian, Thomas, went immediately to sit among the Indians. He spoke with them in muted tones, and sometimes, Smith noted, they did not answer. They were, after all, captives.

Once again, the lieutenant turned to the militiaman with the floppy hat. "What of the others? We heard that there were more."

"We seen ten or twelve more near to this bunch when we come on them, but they took to the woods. They's a few of my boys out tryin' to round 'em up." He leaned to his right and spat as though to punctuate the thought.

"We'll wait until morning to see if more come in."

Then Smith moved into Thomas' line of vision and signaled with a tilt of the head that he wanted a word with him. When the trader rose and approached, Smith drew him away from the group. "What have you learned?" he asked in a low voice.

"They are from Nantahala. The old man is known to me. His name is Tsali. Two of the younger men are his sons. One is a son-in-law. I think the younger woman is his daughter and the boy is her child."

"What about wives of the other men?"

"They are with the bunch that got away. What did the militiaman say about them?"

Smith sighed. "Just that they had slipped away. It's been my experience that once these Indians reach the trees, you can't find them."

In the dying twilight, the trader's face betrayed a troubling thought. "They may come in on their own, if their husbands are here. Tell the guards not to be jumpy tonight."

And so it was so. As darkness fell, a thick, still fog settled about them. There was no light anywhere, save the little that danced from the fire. Later, as most of the party tried to sleep, two women and three small girls simply materialized out of the gloom. When the watch finally realized that they were standing next to him, he jumped with a start.

"At ease!" Smith barked from where he lay near the fire. Catching the eyes of the women, he motioned for them to join the group. As they settled with their men folk, there was a murmur of voices and words that he did not understand, then everything was quiet again.

Tuckasegee River
Cherokee Nation
November 1, 1838

During the night, the rain started again. When he awoke, Lieutenant Smith could hear it dripping steadily in the leaves where the horses were tethered. Oh, Lord, he sighed to himself. That meant that it would be with them all day. As he stirred, others around him stirred. The guard had failed to keep the fire going, so there would be no coffee this morning. Might as well get up.

It was cold. Everywhere, people shivered. The faces of the three enlisted men reflected a foul temper. Mud clung to their uniforms. With a nod to Perry, Smith indicated that the horses be brought over. Might as well get started. It was going to be a long day.

The party of Cherokees began to move as one, as though they knew where they were going. The trader, Thomas, mounted his horse and began to lead them toward the river. As they filed by, Smith scanned them individually. The children would be a problem. They were cold and not walking well. Everything they wore was wet and heavy. The old man of the group seemed to manage; his face was lean and his body was small and slightly stooped, but his steps were firm. There was strength left in him, and in spite of what he faced, he carried himself with dignity. The real problem for the mission would be his wife. She shuffled along the damp earth, one leg obviously not strong, bent under the weight of her wraps. She would bend more as the day went along, Smith judged. He would have to keep an eye on her.

The militiamen stayed behind to search for stragglers in the Lufty area, so he arrayed the regular soldiers that he had brought with him around the party on foot. Spurring his horse, Smith joined Will Thomas at the front. "We will make a slow pace this day."

Thomas made no reply except to look at the officer with disdain that was not there yesterday.

"I take it you don't like this business, Mr. Thomas?"

"You take it correctly, sir."

"What would you have me do, Mr. Thomas?"

Thomas turned in his saddle. "What I would have you do you cannot do because it would be insubordination. What I would have you do I cannot say because I would speak treason. It's best left unsaid."

Smith was shocked by the rebuff. He had known that Thomas' sympathies lay with the Cherokees, but he had not known the extent of it.

The rain drifted straight into their faces as the party slowly skirted the river. Legs moved sluggishly over and around the rocks, and sometimes the trail was so narrow that they had to walk single file to pass. Where the bank was steep, the mounted soldiers rode mostly in the shallows beside the procession, then when the landscape flattened, they moved onto the bank to keep the Indians penned against the river. But no matter what the terrain was like, the going was labored.

It did not take long before the soldiers were barking impatiently to get the people to hurry along. Perry was being particularly hard. He did as he had done with the other party of captives, he walked his horse closer than necessary to the Indians, a reminder that if they faltered they would be stepped on by the beast. For the most part, the trick worked. When Perry came close, the children skittered ahead and even the grown males edged forward faster. Only the old woman did not hasten because she was going as fast as she could go.

Once, when Perry edged close to the woman, Smith gave him a sharp look. No words were said, but after a long moment, the private turned away. Was this soldier seriously thinking about challenging his authority? It was yet another thing to watch.

By ten o'clock, they had made only four miles. Smith called for a rest at the lower end of the big clearing where the burial mound lay. The Indians were silent as they marched by it. But the old man, whom the lieutenant now knew was named Tsali, walked with his head facing the sky, as though he alone was aware that this was the last time that any of them would ever see the mound and was offering a prayer as he passed.

When they halted, the Indians looked exhausted. They huddled together in the rain, with the children in the center to give whatever warmth could be given to them from the massed bodies. It is a job; I have to do it, the lieutenant repeated to himself. He turned from the group and rode ahead along the river so that his men could not see his expression. This was no time to let men like Perry see a chink of doubt. Stopping beside a broad expanse where the river tumbled past jagged rocks, he calculated their progress. In another couple of hours, he would have to get some food into these people. The trail below Big Bear Camp was steep. The soldiers had ridden it without incident yesterday, but these people were on foot and they were exhausted. He had to do something for them or they would begin to fall. The old woman would be first. If she fell, what would the rest of them do?

When the party reached the mouth of Deep Creek, where it spilled its frigid water into the Tuckasegee, a soldier found a shallow spread where the people could ford across. The Indian men carried the children on their backs, but the women, including the old one, walked. Shock of the cold water finally caused some emotion to be registered on the faces of the Cherokees, but when they were all across, they resumed their downcast trudging.

At Big Bear Camp, Smith halted the group in front of a small barn and had Will Thomas lead them in. He negotiated with the White farmer whose name was Welch, to make a stew for the people, and paid him in government money. When the stew had boiled, the people sat on hay and ate from shared bowls, making no sound.

Thomas approached the lieutenant. "How much more are you going to push these people?"

"I've got to get them to the stockade and it's a long way off. Sittin' here don't get us no closer."

"That old woman has got another five-six hours in her. After that, she'll drop. What are you going to do with the rest of these people if she dies on you on the trail?"

Smith had considered this possibility, but did not yet know the answer and it showed on his face.

Thomas went on. "You may not care anything for these people. I do. They are as human as any of us. And marching that old woman to her death is not human."

"Mr. Thomas," the lieutenant countered sharply, "do you think that old woman has a chance in hell of surviving all the way to Oklahoma?"

"No, I don't. But I also don't think that marching her to her grave here is your decision to make."

"What is your point?"

"My point is to see them—all of them—make it to the stockade alive."

Smith nodded, but understood now why the soldiers in his command avoided the trader. They did not like him because he would inevitably make their task more difficult. "They will make it, Mr. Thomas. That is my job."

Getting them moving again was not easy. For the first time in several days, their clothes were drying and the hay was soft. To get them started, the lieutenant hoisted the old woman and a small girl onto his horse. There was a mumbling among the soldiers. Smith caught the look on Pvt. Perry's face that said that he strongly disapproved. It was time for the lieutenant to assert his rank. He pointed at the remaining two children and then at Perry's horse, then turned and started off before the soldier could object. The others followed reluctantly.

From the barn, the party skirted a steep bend in the river, then the banks flattened for a couple of miles and walking was easier. The rain had let up and with bellies full, the people moved with more energy. As the party slowly made its way down the Tuckasegee to where it met with the Little Tennessee, there was a slight increase in animation among the Indians. Once in a while, Smith would glance over his shoulder and catch several of the men cutting their eyes toward each other. The militiamen who had captured this bunch mentioned that most of them lived along the Nantahala, and that was a nearby tributary of the Little Tennessee. Perhaps, nearing familiar ground was making them edgy.

It was then that their first misfortune struck. In

what looked like reasonably solid ground, Will Thomas' horse fell, rolling his leg under its flank and against a rock. When they righted the animal, Thomas was in pain. His leg did not appear to be broken, but it would not support his weight and he sagged with a groan when he tried to stand. Martin and Getty held him up and looked to the lieutenant for instructions.

"How bad is it, Mr. Thomas?"

"Not good," he hissed through clenched teeth. "A sprain, I think."

"Can you ride?"

"I think so. But not for long."

Smith looked up and down the river. There was only one thing to do. "Mr. Thomas, we're going to put you back on your horse and send you back to that farm. They can take you in there, until you are able to get around."

Thomas nodded, and the two troopers boosted him back onto his mount. With a deep breath, he turned the animal and walked it back up the river.

As twilight settled, Smith and the party of captives were nearing a large rock that jutted out into the river when he was startled by a commotion behind him. "Look out. He's got a knife," one of the soldiers shouted.

Stopping the procession, the lieutenant approached the two Cherokee men who were being held by the soldiers. They looked as though they had been caught stealing. When he held out his hand, one produced a long dirk knife without hesitation. Smith tucked it into his belt, and the party proceeded. But the incident left a lingering edginess on the people, as though this one small rebellion, though lost, opened the door to greater rebellion. Now they walked without subservience and when the soldiers looked them in the eye, they looked back.

"Be sharp," Smith called to his men, and almost unthinking, he wrapped the rein of his horse around his fist. Always, he did as he had been trained, and held a loop of the rein in his palm, in case the animal reared. But this time, if there were trouble, he did not want the rein jerked out of his hand. It was a simple thing that would shortly save his life.

As the light was dying, Smith looked for flat land for them to camp that night. He needed to assess their circumstances as well as his own. They had made no more than twelve miles since morning and would not have come as far as they had if he had not put the old woman on his horse. However, barring some major holdup with the original party of captives, he would not catch up to them with this bunch. There would be no grand entrance to the stockade with an impressive gathering of Indians in tow. It would be just another workmanlike mission for him, but nothing outstanding. His colonel would be making no glowing remarks about initiative in his file. How many careers were bogged down by missed opportunities?

At a point along the river where the hillside leveled slightly, the two soldiers that remained mounted rode up the bank. Walking at the head of the party, Smith spun on his heel to look them over. Just then, he saw a small axe fall from the sleeve of the largest male captive and into his hand. "Disarm that man!" he shouted.

There was a moment when no one moved. Then, a glance passed between the old man and the one with the axe. Faster than Smith believed possible, the big man pirouetted and backhanded the axe into the forehead of Pvt. Perry. Before his body hit the ground, the other Indian men attacked the soldiers that remained on horseback. One grabbed the rifle that Pvt. Getty cradled in the crook of his elbow, pulling it toward himself, then reversing and lunging backward toward Getty. The butt struck the soldier in the jaw and he fell from his horse, unconscious. With the rifle in his hand, the brave swung it toward Pvt. Martin, who was still mounted, and fired. The explosion echoed along the steep walls of the gorge. The ball hit Martin in the breastbone, knocking him off his horse.

The rifle report caused Smith's horse to rear, spilling the old woman and little girl onto the ground. Another brave was reaching for Martin's rifle that lay across some rocks near his body. Others hurriedly searched the other bodies for pistols.

Smith had to get out of there. Leaping onto his horse, he tore down the river, hooves clattering over rocks. A second explosion from behind sent a pistol ball for him. It missed. He rode low in the saddle in case more followed, dodging back and forth from the river to the trail.

When he was out of range, he pulled up on the point of a bend and looked back. The Indians were celebrating as they stripped the bodies of the fallen soldiers, their delight a measure of their hatred for their captors. The old man called Tsali stood over them like a sentinel, the bloody axe in his hand now. Unlike the younger ones, there was no celebration on his face, as though he, alone, understood that 7,000 U.S. soldiers would now be looking for them.

Sadness overcame Smith. Surely, there would be no captain's bars for him in his future. He had failed to control the situation and at least two of his men were dead; a third, he was unsure about. He spurred his horse on toward the fort at Almond where help could be found.

Soco Creek
North Carolina
November 14, 1838

Will Thomas still could not sit comfortably on his horse, two weeks after the animal had accidentally rolled on his right leg. His knee was bad, his ankle worse, swollen to twice its normal size. And dismounting brought nightmarish pain when he swung over the saddle and stepped down. To compensate, he relearned to slide down the saddle on his belly and touch the ground gently, the way that he had done as a boy when he was too short to reach the ground from the stirrup. Doing so made him look ridiculous, but he would trade a little ridicule for a lot less pain.

Except for today. The part of him that had become Cherokee since he had come to these mountains as a youth told him that he must show no weakness in what he was about to do. He had to find Euchella, and if he showed pain, Euchella would see his weakness and deem him unworthy—too White—to deal with.

When he started out from the trading post at daylight, rain dripped from the bare limbs of poplar and oak trees, and mist hung in puffs across the valley. Thomas was mindful of his horse's footing and guided it slowly along the rocky edge of Soco Creek. There was just enough light to enable him to see bits of mica and fool's gold reflecting along the sandy bottom. He eased the animal through these areas and avoided the darker spots where silt had settled. The creek was stained a light brown from the rain and ran noisily down the valley, past boulders that were blanketed with a deep green moss. Where the elevation changed abruptly, the water became froth, adding more dampness to the air.

He let the horse set the pace upstream. There was no immediate reason to hurry. He was unsure how Euchella would receive him anyway. Almost a year after the man's wife and child had starved, he still smoldered over it. The few times he had come into the trading post since then, he had the stiff-legged look of a dog that was spoiling for a fight. Will was surprised that someone had not been killed. Harmony was vital to the Cherokees, and since Euchella's family had died during his protest of the removal, it would be natural for him to blame their deaths on the Whites. Harmony demanded balance. Why had no White been killed to atone for it? Perhaps that was the source of the rage that lingered on Euchella's face. He had done nothing to appease the Great Spirit and was, therefore, angry with himself. The look of the man was fearful.

So warned, Thomas continued on up the creek in search of him. Abandoning the cabin that he had shared with his wife, Euchella was said to live with his brother Wachacha and a few others known as the Lufty Band. They drifted somewhere between the valley of Soco Creek and the one formed by the larger river into which the Soco emptied, the Oconaluftee. For six months, this band had been one step ahead of the militia and the army, moving east into Citizen Cherokee lands where they blended in with those Indians who were legal residents of North Carolina, then back west again as their pursuers looked elsewhere for them. They traveled like a pack of coyotes, at night, unseen, silent. What they ate, Will could not imagine, rabbits and squirrels probably.

In his search, Will knew that he might as well

stake out a spot on one of the ridges overlooking Soco Valley and wait. Euchella would eventually pass by. But Will could not wait. Wherever he was, Euchella had to be found soon. All the property that Will was buying for a reservation would need Cherokees to live on it. And for the governments—federal and state—to take the idea seriously, there would have to be a good seed population to occupy the land. But these would have to be people whose loyalty was to the United States, not the Cherokee Nation. John Ross and those he took to Oklahoma would not do. He was too political to be here, and would have loudly and self-righteously reminded the surrounding Whites of what they had so recently done to the Cherokees. In any case, having struggled eight years to send Indians west, the government would never agree to bring any back. The Lufty Band, on the other hand, might suffice, along with the others who were scattered about Alarka, Panther Creek, Hiawassee, Nantahala, and elsewhere. Angry they were. Clannish they were. But silent they were also. The concept of an Indian reservation in the East was novel and therefore fragile. It would need a people who preferred a low profile. The Luftys just might do.

But for this to happen, a chain of events would have to take place. The government must be made to recognize the merit of these people, and find some reason to make a statement of their worth. And since the government in the mountains was now the army, it would be the army that would have to be convinced. Thomas knew at least two-dozen men like himself who sympathized with the Cherokees. They came through his trading post regularly, to buy, to sell, and to commiserate about the times that were changing too fast for them to understand. Like Thomas, their views were simple: The Cherokees had been good neighbors for over thirty years. Why must they leave? As a group, these men would probably put their signatures to a document asking exemptions from removal for the remaining Cherokees. Will would write the document; he was probably the only one who could. But he would not sign it because it would be best that it appear to come spontaneously from the signers. And they must deliver it to the army, in this case, to Col. Foster who was now in charge.

That was part one. Tsali, his sons, and son-in-law had handed the next and most dramatic part to him. *Tsali, Tsali, Tsali, what were you thinking? The soldiers had guns. You had only a couple of flintlocks and an axe. Why did you think that you could fight them? To where did you think you could run? Why did you let them do it? Was it your idea? Did you push the younger ones to do it? Could you not see how this would end?*

Thomas paused his horse for a moment at the mouth of Jenkins Branch. Leaning back in the saddle, he thought about Tsali. He had known the man almost from the time that his mother had brought him to these mountains. Never had there been a hint that the old Cherokee could become violent. He was a fisherman mostly, sometimes walking the nearly twenty miles from Nantahala to Soco to trade fish for flour. Occasionally, his wife, Nancy, would be with him, asking with her eyes for a bit of cloth or a button or some thread. Will remembered that she had been puzzled once by a small washboard; using an old shirt, he had demonstrated how it worked for her, but she had returned it to his hands shyly. It was inconceivable that these people were capable of murder.

The horse lurched and began to walk up the

smaller Jenkins Branch. Will slackened the rein. Why not? The animal had as good an idea as to where Euchella was as he did, so he let it walk.

But his thoughts returned to Tsali. What happened on the Tuckasegee to the captives that Lieutenant Smith was conveying had something to do with Nancy. It was true that one of the dead men, Pvt. Perry, had been aggressive toward her and the others, but not to the point of murder. For a moment, Thomas put himself in Tsali's place: an old fugitive trying to protect his family, driven from his home, then captured and herded like farm animals toward stockades where many of their tribe had died from exposure. Then, if they survived the stockades, who knew what lay in front of them in Oklahoma? Would there be rivers where he could fish? Would he be able to go out of his cabin at night and find firewood lying around for the taking? Would they feel the same spiritual union with the land that they felt here?

Will had no answer to any of these questions, but he had a good idea what it would feel like to be ousted from one's home at the point of a gun and told that from now on it would belong to someone else who had never lived there, never worked the fields, never mended the roof after a storm, and never caught a fish that swam in the river nearby. These hills exhaled the air that these people breathed. Take it from them and they would likely die, as many had already in the stockades. Thomas nodded to himself. That might be worth murder, particularly if it meant saving one's wife from such a fate.

However, because of what Tsali and his sons had done, they must die. The government—particularly the army—could not forgive such a challenge. That would be akin to ignoring insurrection. Even though the vast majority of Indians had been moved west, such an action might encourage more action on the part of those remaining. It had to be stopped quickly.

Already General Scott had written to Col. Foster, directing that, when caught, the men be shot. As far as the army was concerned, the only question that remained was how to catch them? But for Will Thomas there were two more questions: Who was going to do the catching, and who was going to do the shooting? He could see a way that the Cherokees, themselves, could benefit from the present confusion.

The horse followed the creek and soon the broad field turned into a shallow gorge, the slopes of which were covered with a dense, low-growing bamboo. Will swung the animal through a break in the tangle, and rode along the top of the gorge, toward the rising mountains. Soon he reached a knoll where a huge chestnut tree stood, it's porcupine-like burrs littering the ground. Dogs and Indians avoided these things because the spines would penetrate the thickest footpads or moccasins. Squirrels and deer had long since picked over the harvest, so the ground beneath the tree was undisturbed.

Will examined it carefully, memorizing details of leaf, limb, and vine. He scanned the colors and shades of colors, the way things lay together, and the way mushrooms grew from the logs. It was a trick that he had learned as a boy from a tracker. By taking an impression of an untrammeled area, one could spot disturbances elsewhere. What he noticed now was that the rain had made the fallen leaves heavy, and they lay like a sodden quilt on the ground and over downed logs. That's what he would look for, areas where the quilt was disturbed. Eventually, Euchella and his men would have to come out of wherever they were hiding to hunt, and the quilt would be wrinkled.

The flank of the mountain grew steep and the horse labored with the climb. It was well into the morning and he stopped on a slab of granite that stuck out over the valley. Patches of cloud were below him now. Likely, the rain would continue. The air was colder up here, and the steady dripping might turn into ice and make the footing treacherous. He had better push on.

Below the ridge of the mountain, Will worked his way around a thicket of laurel so dense that he could not see into it more than two feet. He doubted that a bear could crawl through it. It could easily hide men, and without a dog to sniff them out, a passerby would never know that they were in there. Will looked it over, but saw no indication that he was being watched, so he moved on. As the ridge came into sight, the wind shifted from the south, blowing into his face and bringing a faint trace of smoke, perhaps from an old fire. He slapped his horse on in anticipation. The animal responded with a snort but finally made it to the top.

For the first time in several hours, Will dismounted, gingerly. The bad leg still did not like to hold his weight and he limped over the ridge to where it sloped down to the south. Suddenly, a crow screamed to announce his presence. Well, he thought, they all know I'm here now. Maybe they will find me.

Down the slope, the quilt of leaves was undisturbed. Disappointed, Will pulled the horse closer and remounted. Then it came to him again, the smell of smoke. Edging forward, he would follow the scent and see where it led.

He continued riding east for a half-hour. There

was no blue plume in the air, so if there had been a fire near here, it would have burned at night, hidden under a ledge or lean-to, just the kind of fire that someone who did not want to be found would build. The crow screamed again, farther off. But as he heard it, Will wondered if, in fact, it were really a crow. The sound was not quite right. Down a saddle on the ridge and up another peak he continued, the animal steady beneath him. Along here, trees were twisted by unending wind, their limbs like the arms of dancers bent toward the sky. As a boy, he had never liked to come up this high. The strange shapes of the trees gave the place a haunted look, and sometimes, when limb touched limb, they squeaked together like someone walking over loose planks. Nowhere could one feel loneliness as one could feel it here.

Just then, an arrow struck the trunk of an oak tree about ten feet in front of the horse. Instinctively, the animal stopped, ears up. Will held his gaze steadily on the arrow. It was more warning than greeting, more greeting than welcome.

From a pine thicket on the south slope of the mountain, a voice emerged. "I did not kill your friend when I had the chance. Why should I not kill you?" It was Euchella's voice.

Will picked his words carefully, remembering that Jonas Jenkins had mentioned seeing Euchella on a hill beside his farm. (It seems that Jonas had been closer to shaking hands with his maker than he had realized.) "I come to talk about the future, not the past."

A reply came quickly. "There is only the past. Your soldiers have taken away the future."

Thomas gripped the back of the saddle and the horn and slowly lowered himself to the ground. When he winced, his face was hidden by the horse. Tying the reins to a branch, he stepped in front of the animal and moved slowly toward the thicket. "There may be a future, there may be a way."

From the stand of trees, Euchella emerged, standing straight, bow in hand. Though his hair and clothes were wet, his eyes burned from a face that was the color of a chestnut. "Will you work one of your Christian miracles and bring the people back? Will you restore my wife and child?"

"I came to speak to you of what I can do, not what I can not do."

The Indian took a step forward and several others emerged behind him, all were wet and sullen. "What is this?"

"There is a day coming when there will be a new Cherokee Nation in these hills. We will be using the money that the government has sent to buy land here for a home for the Principal People."

"Your soldiers have taken the Principal People west to this far place. Will you bring them back?"

"No. This land will be for those who are left."

"There are but a few."

"I know. That is why all who are left are important."

"You talk of buying land when you know that land cannot be 'bought.' People live on the land until they die. Then someone else lives on it."

"I understand the old ways. But this land must be bought one more time, then it will never be bought again. The new Cherokee Nation will be made from a special treaty with the government. It can never be sold again and will belong to the Principal People—and only them—forever."

"You speak to me of treaties when you know that

treaties are what destroyed our nation in the first place?"

Will shrugged, then instantly regretted doing so. It was a White gesture, not Indian, and had no place here. "What have you got to lose? There is nothing here now. You are a hunted man. There is no safe place for you to build a cabin or make a farm. What I'm suggesting could let you reestablish the nation here. Not like it was. Not the same as it was. Not with the people who were here before, but with you and the men who are with you and those few who are still scattered and hiding all over the mountains."

Euchella looked at the men around him, then back at Thomas. "I have heard talk of this, but you did not climb this mountain to tell me this. This I could have found out myself. Why did you come here?"

"I came to tell you that all that I have said will not take place without your help."

"You want me and my brother and the others for this thing you call a reservation?"

"Yes, that, but much more."

"What do you want of Euchella?"

Thomas tried to take a breath without seeming to do so. "I want you to shoot five men."

The wind blew in a cold gust from below, bringing a damp vapor with it and rattling the trees overhead. Euchella took a step back as though he had seen a snake. "Who am I to shoot?"

"Tsali." This was the moment for which he had ridden up the mountain. Euchella would either notch another arrow into his bow and kill him, or else listen to what remained to be said.

From his expression, it was obvious that Euchella struggled with indecision, and that was not a state of mind with which he was comfortable. If, in fact, he had stalked Jonas Jenkins with intent to kill him in retaliation for the deaths of his wife and child, he now faced another moment when instinct clashed with logic. He glared at Thomas for pushing him into this conflict. "My brother speaks of Tsali as Spear Finger," he said finally. "They say that Tsali has set the hearts of the soldiers on fire, that there will be much killing."

Will nodded. "Perhaps. But for now, they cannot catch him—or his sons. They do not know how to catch men who live like rabbits."

"So maybe the Principal People have a small victory in all this."

"At what price? You said yourself that there will be much killing from this. Tsali and his sons have been declared outlaws. I have seen the letter from General Scott. He says that they must be found and shot."

"Then let them find him."

Will shook his head. "They cannot. They have tried. You must do it. You are the only one who can."

The Indian's eyes narrowed. "This was not a wise thing that Tsali did, but it is a thing that I have thought to do myself. The soldiers have chased us for months and we have spoken many times about running no more. This is our home and yet they chase us like we are dogs. We move at night because we know where we are going and the soldiers do not. During the day, we rest where we cannot be seen. But, sometimes it is in the heart of the dog to run no more, to stand and fight. Tsali, himself, has had such a dream. He told me."

"Tsali did what he did. As long as he is out there, there will be no peace for the Principal People.

Until he is dead, the soldiers will remain and every one of you will be hunted. But, if you find him and bring him—and shoot him, according to the rules of the army—they will see you in another light. They will not be threatened by you."

Euchella turned to his brother Wachacha who stood at his right and spoke something that Will could not hear. Then, he turned back to the trader. "You know Tsali is my friend."

"Yes. He is mine, too."

Fort Scott
North Carolina
November 18, 1838

Col. William Stanhope Foster of the 4th Infantry watched the man leave his tent. He knew instinctively that Jonas Jenkins was the only man who could make this whole sorry episode with the Indian Tsali end the way it had to end. Perhaps, the merchant Will Thomas could have done it, but he was injured when his horse fell just before the murders took place and was still hobbling, over two weeks later. He would never have been able to climb where a fugitive Indian would climb. So, it was up to this mild-mannered Jenkins to find Tsali and bring him in. But in his floppy hat and with the distracted—often dreamy look on his face—he just did not look the type to play sheriff.

However, the situation was more complicated than that; just catching the fugitive was the smallest part of what he had to consider. Thomas and Jenkins had come up with a scheme to use a small party of renegade Cherokees from the Oconaluftee area to bring in the fugitives who had murdered two soldiers and wounded a third. It was an intriguing notion, creative, but risky from the Army's standpoint. When the other Indians found the futitives, what would keep them from joining forces and all escaping together? But that was not the end of it. Thomas and Jenkins had come to him, explaining that these Indians from Oconaluftee wanted not only to capture the fugitives, but execute them as well. This group—consisting mainly of about thirty braves, led by a man called Euchella and his brother Wachacha—was a remnant of the Cherokee

Nation that had avoided capture and forced removal. Although they lived within the territory of North Carolina, they were not "citizen Indians" who had signed the land agreement twenty years before. Legally, they were not entitled to stay. However, it was becoming clear that the scouting parties led by Foster's subordinates were not going to catch these fugitives without help. The forest was too dense and the Indians knew where to hide too well to be caught. Perhaps, only another Indian could catch them.

Jenkins and Thomas had come to him two days before, explaining their plan. Jenkins would go with Euchella to help with the roundup and act as liaison to the army. If the colonel would muster him back into the army for a few days (he had been part of the big roundup in May through July), he would see that the fugitives were captured and turned over to the soldiers. Because he was frustrated by the lack of success from the field, Foster did as they suggested. What was there to lose?

And, so far, the scheme was working. Two of the five killers had been caught. Word had come today that two more were almost in hand.

An even more intriguing twist to the story had come in the post today, a petition signed by thirty-one Whites, asking that Euchella's group be allowed to stay in the region after their services of capturing the fugitives had been rendered. The timing of it was most peculiar, too. Neither Jenkin's nor Thomas' signatures were on the petition, yet he could not help but believe that they had something to do with its creation. It was widely known that Thomas was acquiring Indian land, paying cash, even in a time when his business had to be bad. But for what purpose? Was this petition part of his scheme? Foster did not know. The petition was carefully worded. Someone versed in the law may have had a hand in it, and Thomas occasionally practiced law when he was not selling cloth or nails.

This land was filled with intrigues. Keeping the mission clear in his mind would be a struggle.

Wind whipped the tent. The long rain that had begun in September had let up long enough for the rivers to go back down, then it came again, along with an icy fog. This morning the ground and trees wore a crust of ice that sparkled with frigid brittleness. These mountains were already cold as winter approached and the tent afforded little protection from it. Had he wanted to use it, there was space inside each of the four towers of the stockade where Foster could have conducted regimental business. But he had no taste for this place and preferred to do as much from his tent as possible. Maybe the unhappy spirit of John Wool pervaded the fort. After all, he had built it.

Brevet General John Wool—now there was an example for a rising officer to avoid emulating. As the entire army now knew, when Wool served here, he found the narrow path along the cliff of insubordination, and walked it for a year. Full of conscience about what was being done to the Indians, he had all but thumbed his nose at the president. The experience gave his mouth a permanent sour turn. Every soldier was aware of the story: Wool repeatedly asking the Secretary of War to be relieved of a duty that he found morally repugnant, being repeatedly refused, until finally local politicians who wanted the Cherokees gone demanded his removal. Although later exonerated by a board of inquiry, Wool had made an example of himself that no career officer wanted to follow.

Musing on the old gossip, Foster found the similarities between Wool and himself mildly unsettling.

Both had grown up in far northern states, raised by fathers who were ministers. Both had joined the army during the War of 1812, rising rapidly in the officer corps. And both had seen their careers stalemated as political winds shifted and there were no major conflicts to be engaged. As every officer knew, war brought promotion and, since 1814, the closest thing that the army had to war was the nasty little skirmish with the Seminoles in Florida. But that was not a gallant conflict, complete with charges and bombardments that made for good stories and big headlines. Unlike British soldiers, the Seminoles fought a hide-and-seek war, often at night, and never in large groups. They were like the pesky mosquitoes or snakes in the Everglades. You had to kill them one at a time, and that was not the way that the U.S. Army was designed to fight. An officer posted to Florida was likely to find it more blight than benefit to his career.

But that is where the similarities between Wool and Foster ended. Foster had gone to Florida and had, surprisingly, done well, receiving a commendation for his efforts. At the same time, Wool had come to the Smoky Mountains to begin the process of removal of the Cherokees. He was to disarm the Indians and build the forts that would serve as collection points for the trip west. Unfortunately for his reputation, he had fallen into the role of gatekeeper to a would-be land rush, holding back a pack of scavengers who wanted to get their hands on what would soon be free land. In the end, Wool had come to be one of those officers who, when his name came up, caused voices to be lowered.

Foster put down his quill on the letter that he was writing to his wife. Too much introspection made him impatient, restless. Unlike Wool, he was more doer than thinker. Rising from his desk, he adjusted his tunic and stepped outside. A light November wind had carried away the smell of sick and starving people that had permeated the air when he had arrived in the summer. Back then, the air had been almost unbreathable inside the walls. It was worse yet in the camps to the west, those near the navigable rivers that were the primary transport route for the migration. There had been a lot of death in those camps, with the heat and the starvation. All the camps were nothing more than cattle pens, walls to prevent beasts from straying, only these were not beasts that were held inside. And although they were the aboriginal people to the area, the Cherokees were not used to spending weeks on end exposed to brutal sun and now cold, without much food and water. Many died from exposure. Perhaps, Foster surmised, they died from simply being uprooted, like plants from a garden.

He sighed. What a godawful duty this was. John Wool had been right. This was not soldiering. Moving these Indians west was eviction. Foster and the rest of the soldiers had become process servers. Even General Scott found it distasteful, and was glad when he was ordered to leave and go north to the Canadian border. The sooner that the removal was done, the better they would all be. It left him, like Macbeth's wife, feeling contaminated.

Fewer than one hundred holdout Cherokees now stood around fires within the stockade, shrunken within themselves. Foster had seen this kind of withdrawal before in captured animals; once caged, they were unwilling to move, as though blinking their eyes required too much effort and eating was beyond consideration. A few of the Indians looked at him, but most did not. What he represented to them he could not imagine. Perhaps, they were too cold to pay attention. Most wore only shirts, headscarves, and pants of canvas or deerskin. Only a few had coats. Here and there, one stood wrapped in a blanket, but most just hovered by fires. Winter was hinting that it would come early and come hard, and Foster knew that when it did, these people were in for trouble. The supplies promised them were spotty. The food sent to the camps—second rate to begin with—often arrived spoiled, the meat crawling with maggots. Vegetables smelled and were slimy. Sometimes, the merchants who had contracted to supply the camps brought whiskey instead, and this was bartered for a night with a woman or a young girl. He would have stopped that if he could have, but he could not be at more than one stockade at a time.

It all disgusted him. Foster longed for his wife, Betty, and the contentment of their life together. She was the one to whom he told everything, ambition, misery, and even his moments of vague disquiet and self doubt. When they were together, they were playful like children, even though his youth was three decades behind him. Somehow, she made him feel like a pup, and he gladly played the part for her. In their eight years together, she was almost always pregnant. He smiled inwardly at the thought. Since he had joined the army, he had been forced to live two lives, one of the stiff and disciplined soldier, another of the child-husband that so pleased his wife. What pleasure it gave him to make her laugh, or to see admiration in her eyes as he told her a tale of soldiering. Often, it seemed that they were opposite sides of the same person, connected by secret nerve endings of which only they knew. But as close as they were, he had never told her how bad it was in these camps, how much he feared for these people. The actor's face that he wore in front of his men he now wore in his letters to her. Would she know that his words were less than complete? Probably. Would she know that he was compelled to hide the sordid nature of this mission? Probably. Still, he realized as he circled the camp that his letters to her were the only relief he had from the disgust that he felt now.

But being the way he was with her made it possible to be the soldier that he had to be. The love that he felt for her made him more decisive than he had been before they met, and it showed. His work with the Florida Indian troubles had caught the eye of General Scott. As a result, an unspoken agreement had developed between the two men such that if there were a particularly thorny problem in his command, Scott sent Foster to fix it. Which is why he had been called from his post in Baton Rouge to come to North Carolina. This man Tsali had set the country ablaze for revenge and had given the army a black eye. General Scott had called on Foster to fix the problem, and so he would, as soon as Jonas Jenkins caught Tsali.

What to do about the petition from the local Whites—along with the proposal to use the Oconaluftee Cherokees as executioners—he would have to think about. There were confusing precedents there, and he was, after all, paid to be a soldier, not a judge.

Fort Scott
North Carolina
November 22, 1838

William Foster was relieved that he had not been in John Wool's shoes, with orders so repugnant as to make him defy a president. The ones that fell to Foster now he could believe in, with some minor reservations. But in spite of his reservations, he knew that he must not show a hint of doubt about what he was doing.

Four of the five Indians who had murdered the soldiers Perry and Martin had been caught. They—and the old one, Tsali, who was still in hiding—were to appear before a military board of inquiry which would serve the purpose of a trial. They would be shot, of course. The nation and the army demanded it. General Scott even specified punishment in his letter of November 7 to Foster.

The only weakness in the case, the only doubt, was that there was only one witness who was able to testify to the actual events that took place on the bank of the Tuckasegee River. That person was Lieutenant A. J. Smith, commander of the doomed mission. The other surviving soldier was still too ill to testify.

What troubled Foster was Smith, himself. He had gone to considerable lengths to cover up his failure to protect his men. His version of the events of November 1—as reported in a letter to his immediate superior, Lieutenant Larned—could have been written by a lawyer. It was a carefully crafted document. Having studied law himself, Foster recognized the hidden purpose of the document. And that was the problem. The letter told a story that was too well put together to be totally real.

The facts of the matter were indisputable. The Indian, Tsali, aided by sons and a son-in-law, had killed two soldiers of the 2nd Dragoons and disfigured another so badly that his own dog would not recognize him. The killings had taken place while Smith was conveying the party of twelve Indians down the Tuckasegee River to Fort Lindsey, for confinement and eventual transport to the reservation in Oklahoma. But, for an unknown reason, the Cherokees revolted, clubbing one soldier with an axe, then grabbing rifles from the soldiers and killing a second. Throughout the entire process of removing over 16,000 people, they were the only ones to resist. And now how history viewed these events would rest on the testimony of a young career officer who was determined to hide his errors.

All that Foster knew of Lt. Smith boiled down to ambition. He was a middle-of-the-road officer, one determined not to make—or show—mistakes. He was the sort of man who, after a battle, would be one of the few left standing. For that reason he would probably go far just because other men, more moved to action, would be dead. At the end of his career, all the campaign ribbons would be his, but he would have been in the outhouse when the firing started.

However, Smith's career had stumbled on the Tuckasegee with that party of captives. Clearly, he and his men had been surprised. And since Perry had died by having his head split with a Cherokee axe, Foster wondered why Smith had not had the Indians searched when they were first caught. General Scott wanted this matter closed decisively. That's what Foster would do. But the role that Smith played still did not sit right. It was akin to, as his old first sergeant would say, making a stew with spoiled meat. No matter how many onions you put into the pot, it would never taste right. Well, the thing would have to be done anyhow. The public was clamoring for it. Besides, he had the remainder of the Indians within the stockades to transport west. It was time to end this sorry episode. The only real question now was how much of Smith's ineptitude would he expose.

A room within one of the corner blockhouses of the stockade served as a courtroom. With no windows and lit only by oil lamps, the space was dim. The sharp smell of fresh pine rosin from bare timbers mixed with a trace of smoke. Wearing as severe an expression as he could muster, Col. Foster sat in the center of a long table, flanked by Captains McCall and Morris, and Lieutenant Larned who made up the remainder of the board of inquiry. To the left of the table sat a corporal at a desk, taking minutes of the proceedings in a careful handwriting. The witnesses, Lieutenant Smith and the civilian, Will Thomas, sat on a bench to the right. Smith looked nervous. Thomas looked uncomfortable, with his leg wrapped from the accident when his horse rolled on him. A cane lay on the floor beside his chair. The audience was made up of a handful of soldiers and less than a dozen White civilians who knew the defendants to one degree or another. If necessary, they would be called to speak. Although there was great public interest in what happened to these Indians, there was no member of the press in the room. That was just the way Foster wanted it. He had called the board of inquiry unexpectedly, with only four of the five accused men captured. The press had been caught off guard. They took it for granted that nothing would happen until all the fugitives were captured, and with no place for them to stay near the fort, they found accommodations in Knoxville and Athens. So, with the press warm and comfortable elsewhere, the only record of the proceedings would belong to the military. His superiors—particularly General Scott—would understand and appreciate what he was doing. Reporters would have turned this event into a circus of revenge. As it was, it would be handled quietly, and then Foster could get on with the business of transporting the remnants of the tribe to Oklahoma.

For a moment, he scanned the people, looking for the Indian, Euchella, who had caught the fugitives and volunteered to execute them. He was surprised not to find him because Foster knew that he and his band of men were camped outside the stockade.

There was a noise at the door and Foster looked up to see an armed guard enter. He was followed slowly by the four prisoners wearing irons on their ankles and wrists. This was the first time that Foster had seen them, and was taken by how unlike murderers they looked. Cowed by the presence of soldiers, they stared at the floor as they walked. Foster expected defiance from them—if for no other reason than justification for killing the soldiers. But these men were clearly frightened. It did not take much imagination on their part to figure what was about to happen to them. Three of the men were probably between 30 and 40 years old, with grim faces and hands clutched tightly at their waists. They wore loose cotton shirts and pants. One was a large, solid man; he and another had their heads wrapped in bright patterned cloth. The third was much smaller than the other two and his hair hung, uncovered, like a black curtain all the way to his shoulders.

The fourth man was not a man at all, but a boy.

Within his clothes, he trembled as he shuffled into the makeshift courtroom. To Foster, he looked maybe thirteen, although he could have been older. He signaled to the sergeant who led the prisoners to approach his table. "Why is that one held?" he asked, pointing to the boy.

"He was with the killing party, sir. When we captured the others, he was with them. We just assumed . . . ."

Foster cut him off with a nod. The presence of this boy troubled him. He wanted no part of executing one so young and he doubted that General Scott did either. His eyes fell on Will Thomas, seated nearby. "Mr. Thomas, will you approach the bench?" It was not really a question.

Thomas pulled his somewhat cherubic body to his feet and walked unsteadily to the table.

"Mr. Thomas, do you know this boy?"

"Yes, colonel, but not well. His family is of a bunch that lives—lived—on the Nantahala. I know him to be the grandson of the one who is still a fugitive, Tsali. His name is Wasseton."

"Can you guess his age?"

Thomas turned to the Indians in chains and pointed at the boy, then spoke to them in their language that Foster found totally incomprehensible. There was a long silence, followed by a reply from one of the larger captives. Thomas turned back to Foster. "They say he is sixteen."

"Was he with the party that you were escorting when you were injured?"

Thomas nodded. "He was."

Foster exhaled loudly and twirled the gavel that he held in his hand, then looked back at the boy. Justice called for execution of these men; mercy called for recognizing this boy for what he was. But if he were going to do something, he had to do it now, not after these proceedings were concluded. As presiding officer, he had the power to do what he wanted, but putting too much of his own stamp on the proceedings was risky. The thought of overstepping his authority brought back the memory of John Wool. But he was not John Wool. John Wool would have fumed and dithered over the issue, and perhaps written a letter of complaint to the War Department. William Stanhope Foster did not dither.

"Sergeant, cut that boy loose from the others and return him to where the others are kept." Then, in an aside to the stenographer, he said, "Make note, that in consideration of this person's age, he is being excused from these proceedings and any sentence that results from them." In a glance to Thomas, he saw a faint smile on the face of the merchant.

In his letter of November 7, General Scott had already said that these men were to be shot. So, the purpose of this inquiry was not to find guilt, but rather to support the sentence. There would be only two witnesses, Smith and Thomas. For the purpose of making the case solid, Foster would have Thomas testify first. But this brought up another unsettling peculiarity. The defendants had the right to question the witnesses. But, as Foster understood, they spoke little if any English. Thus, Thomas, who was the only qualified translator, would have to give his testimony in both English and Cherokee, then answer any questions from the accused in Cherokee and translate his replies back into English. Also, since Thomas was the only other qualified lawyer in the room, it would fall to him to act as spokesman for the Indians. It could prove to be a very tortured process.

Foster banged his gavel and called the tribunal to order. To the soldier who escorted the prisoners, he ordered, "Sergeant, identify your prisoners."

The soldier pulled a piece of paper from his tunic and cleared his throat. "They go by various names, sir, both Indian and White. Which ones do you want me to use?"

"All of them, sergeant."

"Yes, sir. The first one here, the largest, is known as . . . I can't pronounce the Indian, sir."

"Spell it."

"C-h-u-t-e-q-u-u-t-l-u-t-l-i-h. In English, he is known as Big George or Nantahala George." Pointing to the second man, he went on. "This one is C-a-n-an-t-u-t-l-a-g-a, or Nantahala Jake. The third man is L-a-u-i-n-n-i-h, or Lowen."

"And sergeant, for the record, what is the name of the one who remains a fugitive?"

"His name is T-s-a-l-i, or Charley."

To Captain McCall, the colonel instructed that he read the charges.

McCall pulled a paper before him. "On the afternoon of November 1, 1838, while being escorted by Lieutenant A. J. Smith, Corporal Martin, and privates Perry and Getty of the 2nd Dragoons, these prisoners did render grievous bodily harm to the aforementioned enlisted men, killing Martin and Perry and gravely wounding Getty. An attempt on the life of Lieutenant Smith was made also, but he was afforded escape by the spirited action of his horse. Thus, these men stand charged with two counts of murder and two counts of attempted murder of U.S. Army personnel in the conduct of their duty."

After a moment of silence for this to digest, the colonel outlined the purpose of the board and scope of the inquiry. "The facts of this case are clear. On November 1 of this year, these men deliberately and willfully murdered two soldiers of the United States Army, did grievous harm to a third, and attempted to murder a fourth in the conduct of their duty. Guilt of these individuals is not in doubt. Two of them were apprehended soon after the crime, and the third was apprehended shortly thereafter. What we are about here today is to ascertain how the events of that day took place, and to pass sentence on these men."

Will Thomas was called to the witness stand and was sworn in.

"Mr. Thomas, did you witness the events of November 1?"

"No, sir, I experienced an accident with my horse and could not accompany the party much past the place known as Big Bear's Camp."

"But you were with them up to that point?"

"Yes, I was."

"Were the men seated before you part of the group of captives?"

"Yes."

"Had they displayed any hostility up to the time that you broke from the party?"

"No. None."

"Did you have any sense that they were rebellious or could be dangerous?"

"No. I saw nothing like that."

"In the time that you were still with the party, did you see anything that might suggest that the Indians were being mistreated?"

Thomas did not speak for a moment. When he did, he chose his words carefully. "Lt. Smith was pressed for time, and a few of the old ones and young ones could not move fast. As I remember, he put

Tsali's wife, Nancy, on his horse, along with one of the little children, so they could move faster."

"Were they mistreated in any way?"

"One of the privates, I believe it was Perry, seemed hostile toward them. He kept walking his horse close to them to hurry them on."

"What did Lt. Smith do about that?"

"He cautioned the man, as I remember."

"Was that the end of it?"

"Yes, as I recall."

"Would you translate your testimony to the prisoners?"

Thomas turned to the Indians and spoke for a time in their language. Then, he paused and seemed to ask them a question. There was another long pause, then the first man shook his head. Thomas turned back to the board of officers. "I spoke to them of what I had said, and asked if they had questions about my testimony. It appears that they do not."

Foster nodded. "That being the case, you may step down. But I would ask you to take a chair near the prisoners so that you may more immediately translate what follows."

Lieutenant Smith was called to the stand. Unless something unexpected happened, he would be the final witness. Foster had thought about including the testimony of the soldiers who had come to Smith's rescue after this escape from the ambush, but decided that they could add nothing more than what Will Thomas had provided—corroborative testimony concerning the whereabouts of some of the murderers. That could go on forever, and if anything, be more harmful to Smith's reputation. Personally, Foster felt ambivalent about protecting Smith's reputation, but the more that came out about dereliction of duty, the more confused the final outcome of the inquiry would be. Thus, he decided to let all the weight of the inquiry rest on Smith's answers alone.

"Lt. Smith, would you describe the events of October 31 and November 1 of this year that are in question before this board?"

Smith nodded and pulled a slip of paper from his tunic and began to read from it. But this irritated Foster. "In your own words, lieutenant."

"These are my words, sir," Smith said, waving the paper in the air.

"As you recall the events from memory, Mr. Smith," Foster corrected, "not from some precomposed document. This board wants to know what you remember, not how well you write."

Stung, Smith put the paper back into his tunic. "I was leading a party of captives that had been turned over to my command, down the Little Tennessee River, for the purpose of securing them at Fort Lindsey. We were overtaken by a rider who said that another group of Indians was rounded up by militia, up on the Oconaluftee River. I left the party that I was with and took Corporal Martin and Privates Perry and Getty—along with Mr. Thomas—with me to see if we could bring in this new bunch."

"How many Indians were involved?"

"At the time, I did not know exactly. The rider said that there could be as many as twenty. They were located upriver, almost where the Oconaluftee joins the Tuckasegee. By the time we got there, it was nearly night. We found the party, but there was only about six or seven fugitives at the time."

"So, where were the others?"

"The militiamen had been chasing them and they were scattered. What they had at the time were several men, two women and one boy. We made camp for the night and it began to rain. Sometime during the night, some women and children walked into the camp."

Something odd in Smith's voice caused Foster to probe the point. "They were not challenged by your guards?"

"No."

"Why not?"

"With the rain, there was a thick fog. The guards did not see them, and these people move silently."

"Do you think that you should have doubled the guard?"

"At the time, there seemed to be no need to. There had been no hostilities with these people. I posted the guard that was normal for the circumstances."

"What was the total number of captives when this second group arrived?"

"Twelve."

"Were any of these people known to be armed?"

"Two of the men carried rifles. We took off the locks, and took what they had by way of powder and ball. Corporal Martin kept these on him."

"What did you do the next morning?"

"When it became obvious that no more Indians were coming in, we packed up and started down the river."

"What became of the militiamen who were there?"

"They went to look for more Indians. As I said, they thought that there was a total of about twenty in this group, so they thought that they might find more."

"We have heard testimony from Mr. Thomas that

at least one of your men—Pvt. Perry—showed impatience with the slow pace of the party, and tried on several occasions to hurry them along."

"We weren't moving fast. One old woman was particularly slow. She couldn't walk well and everyone was wet from sleeping in the rain. Their clothes must have been heavy. Pvt. Perry edged up behind some of the people with his horse. I told him to stop doing that."

"Did he comply?"

"Yes."

"What happened in the afternoon?"

"We had gone six, maybe seven miles when we stopped at a farm at a settlement called Big Bear, to see if we could get something to eat. The farmer fixed a kettle of stew and afterward, I thought to get the party moving again."

"Was there some resistance to going on?"

"Yes. The people did not want to go farther. Mr. Thomas argued about this. He feared for the life of the old woman."

"But you pushed on anyhow?"

"Yes. We were under orders to get all these people down river as soon as possible. To make better time, I put the old woman and one of the children on my horse."

"Was it about this time that Mr. Thomas had his accident?"

"Shortly after we left the farm, along side the river. His horse fell. I feared that his leg was broken, but after a time, he was able to ride again."

"So you continued down the river."

"Yes. It was not long after that happened that I saw one of the male captives with a dirk knife in his hand."

"What did you do then?"

"I ordered the party stopped and the knife to be taken from him."

"Where had the knife been concealed?"

"It may have been up his sleeve or it may have been on one of the women. I do not know because none were wearing knives that I could see."

Foster paused to consider the direction in which he wanted to take the inquiry. The other members of the board were free to ask their own questions, but each understood that it was Foster's show. If Foster followed the line of Smith's negligence, he could do irreparable damage to the man's career. In addition, it might not serve the purpose of concluding this inquiry neatly as Gen. Scott had expressly wished. On the other hand, Smith had exposed his men to what turned out to be serious danger. A knife-wielding captive was clear evidence of that. And his neglect had led to the death of two soldiers and the disfigurement of a third. There must be rebuke in this inquiry for Smith. "Given the presence of the knife, Lieutenant, why did you not have the remainder of the party searched?"

There was silence in the room. It was obvious from Smith's face that this was the question that he did not want asked.

"Did you hear the question Lieutenant? I repeat, why did you not search the entire party at that point?"

"I—I assumed that it would not be necessary."

"Mr. Smith, how long after you took the knife from the man did the others attack?"

"A matter of some minutes . . . maybe five, six."

"So, it was clear that the presence of the knife was a precursor to armed resistance."

"In hindsight, yes," Smith replied stiffly.

"It is clear that hindsight should have been foresight, Lieutenant," the colonel retorted. "But for your slothfulness in this matter, two soldiers would be alive today, we would not be sending parties into the mountains in search of fugitives, and it would not be necessary to conduct this fact-finding inquiry."

"What would you have me do, sir?"

"Act like an officer and protect your men," Foster shot back. Again, his words seemed to stop all movement in the room. That was as much as he wanted to say about Smith's conduct. There would be no written reprimand to go into his file, only this sharp comment to remain in the memories of the other soldiers in this command. In the future, they would be careful when they served with Smith. But now it was time to go on. "What happened after you found the knife, Lieutenant?"

"We pressed on for a few minutes, until I glanced around to see an axe in the hand of the first prisoner there," he said, pointing to Nantahala George. "I shouted an order to take the axe, but he chose that moment to attack, and split Pvt. Perry's head with it." Then indicating Nantahala Jake, he continued, "That one grabbed the muzzle of Pvt. Getty's rifle and shoved it into his face, then turned the rifle on Cpl. Martin and shot him."

"What did you do at this time?"

"I tried to draw my pistol, but my horse reared when the rifle discharged and knocked it out of my hands. When I saw the men going for Martin's rifle, I shoved the old woman off my horse and escaped down river."

"Did they fire at you?"

"Yes, when I was about thirty yards away. I heard the report and the ball as it went over my head."

Foster sat back. This was the testimony that he needed to get on paper. It was enough to ensure the execution of these three men—and the old one when he was caught. There was little more to be said, except to explain why Pvt. Getty had been left alive by the Indians. "I understand that shortly afterward you were able to return to the scene of the crime with a rescue party."

"I was. There was another detail down the river and they heard the shots and came at a gallop. We returned and the fugitives scattered into the woods."

"Were you able to capture any of them?" Foster knew the obvious answer to the question, but wanted to hear what Smith would say.

"No. They disappeared on foot and we could not follow them. The area is covered by dense growth and is too steep for horses."

"In what condition did you find your men?"

For the first time, Smith showed a flicker of regret. "Perry and Martin were dead. Getty was in bad shape, but could travel. We were able to put him on a horse and bring him out."

Foster asked for questions and when there were none, he called a recess and retired to his tent to think and write the sentence to match the judgment that he was certain would be forthcoming from the board. They would have no problem carrying out General Scott's wishes that these men "*. . . be shot down.*" Pardoning the boy had been a good thing, but the other three—and Tsali, when they caught him—would have to pay the price of their actions. The demands of honor, security, and tranquillity must be satisfied.

His hand shook a little as he began to write. He had never written an order such as this one, but he knew what to say. The prisoners would be executed tomorrow, by firing squad, in the manner prescribed in the Manual of Uniform Code of Military Justice. Prisoners would be bound and blindfolded. Two men would be assigned to shoot each man, one aiming for the head, the other for the heart. Death would be swift.

There was a rattling outside the tent. "Colonel, sir?"

"Enter."

Will Thomas limped in, followed by the militiaman Jenkins. In a moment, the tent flap opened again and a tall Cherokee entered. From the look in his eyes, Foster was tempted to reach for his pistol. Most of these Indians hid their thoughts well, but from the look of this one it was clear that he lived with rage. Tension filled the tent. Foster motioned for them to be seated, but it did little to ease the sense of hostility in the air.

Will Thomas spoke first. "Colonel, as you recall, when we proposed that the Lufty Cherokees be allowed to bring in the murderers, we also suggested that they be allowed to handle the executions."

Foster stared at the Indian as he answered Thomas. "I remember. But I still do not understand your reasoning."

Thomas was momentarily flustered by the directness. "The point . . . Colonel, is to give these people an act of responsibility to regain some control over their lives. Those who are left here must begin again with something. They were as horrified by the murders as the army was. This could have resulted in wholesale reprisals by White settlers. Every remaining Cherokee could have been declared an outlaw and wiped out. Allowing the Lufty Cherokees to carry out the executions would be a 'statement of intent' on their part to manage their affairs in the future."

Foster sat back. He felt surrounded by lawyers. Just how much he could trust Will Thomas in this situation he was not sure. Thomas had another, undeclared motive for his involvement in these executions. Revenge? Not likely. He could not show such obvious affection for these people and hold a blood lust for them at the same time. It was something else. The executions would be part of some greater plan. But what was it? If the two of them played a card game, this critical card remained face down on the table.

The soldier turned his attention to the Cherokee. The dark color of youth had gone from the man's hair, but it was not yet gray. Even seated, it was obvious that his body was lean and straight. But his eyes were the arresting parts. They seemed filled with an unsatisfied need for revenge, as though the man had seen too much death, and, like logs jammed in a river, the memories would not move on. "What is your interest in this, sir?" Foster asked the Cherokee.

Thomas spoke for him, presuming that the colonel would understand that his words needed to be translated. "His name is Euchella. He understands the need to begin again. Word here is that the murderers have become like a mythological figure to them, one they call Spear-Finger, who was condemned to die because she brought shame on the tribe. They feel the need to erase the shame."

All this was plausible to Foster, if a little theatrical. But in any case, he could not see where the army would object. What about General Scott? Probably he would not object, either. The general liked to have things concluded neatly. "You have my permission to act on the army's behalf, gentlemen. Where will these executions take place?"

For the first time the Indian spoke. He seemed to handle the language almost as well as the White man. "We will go to the place where the rivers come together, the Tuckasegee and the Little Tennessee. It will be done there."

Later, when Foster crossed the courtyard back to the room in the blockhouse, he avoided looking at the eyes that followed him. Sitting behind the table again, he reconvened the board meeting.

"Mr. Thomas, will you have the prisoners stand." Thomas spoke in Cherokee to the three men in chains, and slowly they got to their feet.

To the three other members of the board of inquiry, he asked for their conclusions. "Captain McCall?"

"Guilty."

"Captain Morris?"

"Guilty."

"Lieutenant Larned?"

"Guilty."

"Make note that the chair also votes *guilty*."

The colonel paused for a moment to spread the paper that he had composed in his tent. "It is the finding of this military board of inquiry that the three of you—known as Nantahala Jake, Nantahala George, Lowen, as well as the one known as Charley—have been found guilty of the crime of murder of United States Army personnel in the conduct of their duty.

"The three of you will be taken forthwith from this place and be executed by firing squad in accordance with the rules of the United States Code of Military Justice. Said execution will take place tomorrow, November 23, 1838, at the confluence of the Little Tennessee and Tuckasegee rivers. May your God have mercy on you.

"The remaining fugitive—the one known as Charley—is to be similarly executed upon his capture.

"This board of inquiry is concluded."

Fort Scott
North Carolina
November 23, 1838

The day before, Euchella had been inside the stockade that the White men called Fort Scott. He would not go in again, not this one, nor any of the other stockades that soldiers had built, in the Snowbirds and beside the Valley and Little Tennessee Rivers. High walls were made of logs cut and laid on their ends so that they stood straight up. At the corners were blockhouses for guards, and one where they kept three prisoners, men whom Euchella knew well. With Will Thomas and Jonas Jenkins, he had been inside to talk with Col. Foster. The four men had sat in a tent pitched on the bare ground in the middle of the stockade and spoke of Tsali, his sons, and his son-in-law. The White men had talked in long, rambling words—some of which Euchella had not understood—but it was clear that how they said a thing was more important than what they said. This was common to them, their words like the beautiful arcs of rainbows in the sky that follow a storm, but have no substance. Now, however, Euchella knew that he had no choice but to accept their words. If they were true, then he and his band would be free—or as free as they would ever be on this reservation that Will Thomas described. If not, then he would be hunted again as he had been since summer, or shot. Time would tell. But he was not here because he trusted them. This was necessity.

No matter what, though, he would not go back inside a stockade, nor would he take his men in there. Yesterday, he had seen the Cherokees who were inside, waiting to go west. They stood like chickens in a cage; whatever they had before that had made them Cherokee was gone. The images made something inside his head scream like the cry of a crow. Euchella would rather sleep out here, under a lean-to, on a pile of wet broom sage than to go inside the stockade again.

On this morning when he awoke, his clothes smelled of smoke from the campfire. Clouds parted and a small patch of blue passed overhead. For a moment, he felt free again as he had been as a young man. There were no soldiers. There was no removal. His wife and daughter were still alive. Men hunted together and women tended gardens together. Then the clouds closed and the moment passed. He remembered why he was here, with his brother and the others, but the meaning—in the Cherokee way—was unclear. The clouds and the sky and the memories were like symbols in a dream that never came together as a picture in his head. As a boy, he had sat on the mountain overlooking the valley of the Soco and tried very hard to think of what the passing shapes and the slanting rays of light above him must mean. What did they foretell? Was a birth about to happen? Would snow come early? Would the beans and the squash be poor or plentiful? He would try to force his head to hear what the spirits were saying, but always the cloud would drift on before he could fathom its meaning. Manhood had made him no wiser. When he sat in the frozen valley of the Snowbirds last year, he watched the sky, hoping for a sign to be made clear to him. For days he held to his place within a laurel thicket, watching the eastward drift of clouds. He sat so still that rabbits came and went in front of him without sensing his presence. But no sign appeared, even as his family was starving. No feeling or sense or dream told him to go home; the only dream he had was the one of a man covered in ashes and that made no sense to him. It was the last dream that he could remember. Not until he saw the old man Tsali approach through the snow did he know that something was wrong. He must accept that no part of him would ever be a shaman. The best that he could be was only a warrior.

Was that enough? On this day, when he and the men with him were about to become something other than Cherokees, even that was unclear. They would act like warriors, but they would kill like White men. Harmony would not be restored in the Cherokee way, but the White way. The colonel, who sat in his tent in the stockade, required that the killing be done as the army would do it. Euchella preferred to do it, as he had witnessed as a youth, in the middle of a village so that all could see that balance was restored. But there were no villages anymore, and the few Cherokees who remained were scattered, hiding, or on the run from the army, like the Luftys. Still, he struggled with the thought of the executions. It was true that Tsali, Canantutlaga, Lau in nih, and Chutequutlutlih had endangered those left by killing the two soldiers. In his lifetime, Euchella could not remember the curse of Spear Finger being laid on any of his people. But Tsali had become the mad dog of his own dream, and the people openly called him Spear Finger. He would have to die now, even if the army had not wanted him dead. A mad dog could not be allowed to live among the people. So, as Euchella had explained to the other members of his band, executing the three men who were inside the stockade—and then Tsali when they caught him—would restore harmony. He tried to sound like a chief as he spoke the words, but there was the feeling of compromise in this, as though they were not doing it for harmony alone, but for some other, hidden reason. Now, instead of coming to understand what the clouds and dreams and spirits spoke, he, himself, was beginning to sound like a White man.

Euchella rose, feeling unclean in a way that no pure smell of smoke could hide. Whatever the arrangement was between Thomas and Col. Foster about their freedom, it would all begin with the executions. The men of Tsali's family that the Luftys captured two days before on the Nantahala knew that they were dead men from the moment they were surrounded. But they came with them to be turned over to soldiers with little protest, as though the life had gone out of them already. They knew that they were Spear-Finger, too. Tsali would know it as well when he saw Euchella.

The gate of the stockade opened slightly, and Jonas Jenkins and Will Thomas emerged. No soldiers followed as they approached the large fire ring where the group of thirty Lufty warriors gathered. Thomas came directly up to Euchella. For a moment, they stood reading each other's faces. The two men had spent many years together and would have believed, before this, that they knew each other well. But now they stood assessing each other as strangers.

"You will do this thing?" the trader asked.

Euchella replied with a single nod.

"Jenkins and I will go with you, and then when it is done, he will go on with you to find Tsali."

Euchella was surprised. "No soldiers?"

"No. They are leaving here. They will take the remaining people inside to the boats that will take them west. What we do here today is up to us. The colonel is writing a letter to General Scott saying that the thing is done—and also saying that he is allowing the Luftys and the others who were not captured to stay here. He will explain how you have helped the army. It will go out with the post rider when they leave the fort."

That was the thing that Euchella had not wanted to hear and he felt his body stiffen, but before he could reply, the stockade gate swung wide, pushing over clumps of hoar frost as it opened. A squad of soldiers surrounded the three Indian prisoners and nudged them forward. Euchella watched Canantutlaga, Lau in nih, and Chutequutlutlih walk haltingly, their legs in irons.

Jonas Jenkins stepped forward. "Take off their chains. They have a long way to walk."

The sergeant in charge hesitated. He was unused to taking orders from a civilian, particularly one with a moonstruck expression and reedy voice. He looked to Thomas.

"Do it," confirmed the merchant.

Soldiers bent to unfasten the leg irons, then stood up. For a moment, they, too, seemed unsure of what to do as though they were reluctant to let go of the murderers who had killed their companions. Then, as if prompted by a silent signal, they turned and moved back inside the stockade. Will Thomas followed the soldiers, then returned shortly, riding his horse. "Now it's up to you," he said to Euchella.

The tall Indian picked up the blanket on which he slept, and took his flintlock from where it rested against a tree. His brother and the others followed his example. Collectively, the party began to move down the Little Tennessee River, past wide sweeping bends where the water ran shallow. In the morning cold, mist hung over the river, giving the strata of rocks that traversed it a soft appearance. Mostly, the noise of rushing water covered their footsteps, but beside sections where it ran slow and deep, the sound of a large group of men moving at the same pace drummed in the trees above them.

This river eased along like an old man, Euchella thought, with steady purpose, without the rush and youthful impertinence of the Nantahala or even the Oconaluftee. He preferred to think about the river, rather than the three men who followed, but thoughts of them kept intruding into his mind. He had picked the spot where they would die—where the Tuckasegee and the Little Tennessee ran together—so that their spirits could choose which way they wanted to go in the next life. Up river would take them back to one of the old villages of the Principal People. Down river would take them west, where all the others had gone.

Euchella did not look over his shoulder. There was nothing more to say to them. They had all hunted together at one time or another; Chutequutlutlih and he had even killed a bear together. And every man in the party—White included—had eaten fish from Tsali's traps. No more. This was the last of those days, and just as the river could not turn around and flow up hill, they could not go back to those days. Perhaps, after today, there would be some other future for himself and the other Principal People, but Euchella could not imagine what it would be.

After many hours of walking, he could see the gently sloping knoll that divided the two rivers. Crossing over a small creek, they began to climb to the rise. No one had told the three men where they would be killed, but they seemed to know. What energy they had regained in the trek down the river went out of them, and they stood among the others, unmoving. Will Thomas got down from his horse and took a rope from his saddle and the three were tied to separate trees. Jonas Jenkins produced blindfolds from his pocket and went up to each man, asking if he had anything to say. None did, and he tied the blindfolds on, one by one. When he was done, Thomas stepped in to read some unfamiliar words from the book that the Christian preachers used, then stepped aside. Two of the Lufty braves had been assigned to shoot each prisoner, one aiming for the head and one aiming for the heart. Euchella took up his position as the head shooter on Chutequutlutlih. Thomas took charge and barked the instructions.

"Ready!" Rifles rose to shoulders.

With a head like the bear that they had killed, Chutequutlutlih was the strongest man that Euchella knew, far stronger than himself, with a body like the trunk of a stunted oak that grew high up. He could lift stones from the river that no one else could move. More than once, Euchella had seen him hold one over his head, then, grinning, toss it at anyone standing nearby. Big as he was, there was a child inside him.

"Aim!" Hammers cocked.

In the ball games between their villages, no one from the Oconaluftee team wanted to be caught by Chutequutlutlih when they played the Nantahala village. Ears and cheeks had been torn and ribs caved in by the force of his stick. And his grip could break another's hand. Fortunately, Chutequutlutlih was not fast and could be outrun. Euchella had known him since he had come to Nantahala from the Snowbirds to marry Tsali's daughter. It was he who had described the long, high valley to which Euchella had fled last year. He described the thickets and overhangs where a man could hide. His description had been encouraging.

"Fire!" The hilltop erupted.

The body of Chutequutlutlih lurched backward against the tree, head snapping against the bark, then slowly slumped over the restraining rope. As metal slugs ripped through him, what Euchella knew of the man seemed to depart by the time the echo of the shots came back to them from across the river. Where he had stood, there was now a dark stain on the bark of the tree.

For a long time, no one moved. Even those of the Luftys who did no shooting were transformed by what they had collectively done. A second echo of the rifles reverberated from another direction. Finally, Thomas crossed to where the dead men slumped down and cut the ropes, allowing the bodies to slip to the ground. "If you and your riflemen go for Tsali, the rest of us will bury these."

Euchella breathed hard as he realized that everyone was waiting for him to do something. Because of this, he would be the recognized leader now of those who remained on the old tribal lands. Only one thing remained to be done. Nodding to the others with rifles, he picked up his blanket and set off for Deep Creek, with Jonas Jenkins trailing behind.

Deep Creek
Cherokee Nation
November 25, 1838

It was one of Jonas Jenkin's peculiarities that he so much loved the rivers and the creeks in these mountains. He was not alone in this feeling, he knew. Will Thomas had often talked of his fascination with Soco Creek. But for Jonas, it was not just admiration for their beauty and energy, but it was also a sense of belonging that he never bothered to define. That was probably just as well. If he had words to describe this feeling, then he would have tried to explain it to someone . . . his wife, or perhaps, Thomas . . . and they would have thought him even more odd than they already did.

This morning, it was beside another stream—a place called Deep Creek—that Jonas camped, reflecting on all the turmoil that had taken place in these mountains since he had arrived from Virginia. It was a bitter reality that sleep had mercifully enabled him to forget for a short time. But as soon as he opened his eyes and felt the damp earth beneath him, it came back.

Euchella was with him again as he had been on so many mornings beside the Soco. Only now the feeling of companionship that they had shared years before was gone. Euchella was grown to full manhood and had changed from the serious, but approachable, little boy who had possessed an unspoken curiosity about White men. No longer pursuing imaginary bears and deer, he was now a tall, lean man with hard creases around his eyes. But what had really changed the most was his manner. There was now a dangerous quality about him that imparted a prickly sensation in those close by, the same sensation that Jonas experienced when he handled gunpowder.

Euchella sat on his blanket across the campground from Jonas, slowly eating something that he'd pulled from a pouch. Jonas guessed that it was cornbread or just raw meal. His face betrayed no emotion, nor even recognition that his old friend was also awake. Only the sound of the fast running water filled the silence between them.

Jonas shifted his attention to the creek. He knew the smell of this stream, too, like that of the damp earth that fed it from ten thousand trickles along the valley walls. The stream was not big here—a man could jump across it—but it made up in noise what it lacked in size, in a hurry to get down to the flat meadows where the land leveled out.

The rains of November had stopped finally, but everywhere the ground was soaked. Jonas lifted himself off his blanket, feeling as though he would never know what it was like to be dry. He had not seen his cabin or Juliet for ten days, since he had gotten word through Will Thomas that Col. Foster wanted him back in the militia for a special mission. Jonas had known what the mission would be even before he was told; the plan that he and Thomas had discussed concerning an eventual reservation was beginning to work out. But then, everyone knew about Tsali and what he had done. Now, Tsali had become part of it.

When he met the colonel and Will Thomas at the post by the Little Tennessee River, Jonas understood the gravity of the mission. The words coming from the soldier sounded too serious to come from one who looked so kind. Except for the voice, the colonel had the face of a schoolteacher, not too many years out of college. Jonas suspected that he was much older than he appeared to be. "I have orders from General Scott to capture and execute this man Tsali. He and his group, as you know, murdered two soldiers. A third was injured and may not survive." The colonel shifted uncomfortably in his chair behind a small writing table. "You may also know that we've tried to run this man Tsali, or as we call him, Charley, to ground, but he's evaded us. Our scouts are pretty sure that they know where he is, but there's no way that a squad of soldiers can get in there on horseback to root him out." He paused again. Jonas sensed that there was something about this situation that the young colonel did not like. "I want you to go with the Oconaluftee Band because you know these people better than anyone else. You will be the government presence there, see that what must be done gets done."

With a voice that was not quite his own, Jonas asked, "What is to be done, sir?"

"All of them are to be caught and executed. As soon as we have a hearing."

There was a long silence between them. When Thomas posed the idea that the Oconaluftee Band be not only the hunters but also the executioners, Jonas had reacted badly. It had the smell of "deal" all over it. And if it were a deal, it was a poor deal for the Indians, trading the incompetence of the army in locating Tsali for a small piece of the land that already belonged to them. But later, after talking with Euchella, Jonas received a huge shock. The Indians were more than willing to do this. That's when Euchella told Jonas about Spear-Finger. It was a story that Jonas had never heard. Tsali had become a thing of which they must rid themselves. They sure were full of surprises, Jonas realized.

As he rested on one elbow and stared at Euchella, he sensed that the long nightmare was almost over. Three men had been executed the day before yesterday. Now they waited for the decision of the last fugitive. Would he come in willingly to be shot, or were Jonas and the Luftys going to have to climb this mountain and root him out of his hole like a groundhog? They would just have to wait and see.

Deep Creek
Cherokee Nation
November 25, 1838

While his pursuers warmed themselves beside a campfire down the mountain, Tsali sat at sunrise, awaiting an answer. His choices were simple: He could stay here and move around and confuse them and hold out for a long time. He could live up in these mountains and eat things that the old people of the far distant past used to eat in winter, before his people became farmers. He could live like a warrior because, truly, Tsali was at war with the United States and the men in blue uniforms, and, now, the Cherokee braves who did their work for them. If he did this, his wife would worry and live a hard life because she would be a constant reminder to the rest of the Principal People of their suffering. On the other hand, he could turn himself in and be shot and perhaps the soldiers would go away and what was left of his family would live in peace, even if it had to be in this new place in the west. He could see the choices clearly, but he was not sure that he believed in either of them. Both options seemed unreal, but he did not know why. Perhaps, he just did not understand it. For a moment, Tsali shamed himself. He was sixty years old. His family had counted on wisdom from him in the past. His wisdom must not fail him now.

Whatever he decided to do, he would die soon, either by bullet or starvation. He was not strong enough to live long in this cave. As a young man, he had counted his life in summers, as in his fifteenth summer he had killed his first bear. But as years and generations rolled past, Tsali knew that winters were what subtracted the time left to a man. And his winters had accumulated to the point that they weighed on him like a too-heavy cloak, pressing him ever closer to the earth. Perhaps, that was the only wisdom to be had, that one lived a life without care in the sun and humid nights of the summer until the weight of the winters that you endured bore down and drew you into the earth. Had he been counting the wrong season all this time?

The mist in the valley below cleared and in the distance Tsali could see the smoke from the fire where Euchella camped. That was when he remembered the dream. It was the same dream that had haunted him for a half-dozen years. It must have come again last night, after he had eaten some dried corn and settled under the rock ledge, or maybe it had been the night before. He couldn't remember so well any more, but now the dream came back to him, clear now. There was a tall man in uniform on horseback, riding slowly away from Tsali. The uniform was fancy and there were shiny things on his shoulders, and bright buttons, the clothes of a highborn man, like a chief, perhaps. But as he rode away, he looked back at Tsali and Tsali could see tears on his face that ran all the way into his moustache. Tsali was struck by this; he had never seen a grown man weep and he thought that it must be a thing peculiar to White men. The soldier continued to stare at Tsali as he rode away and finally disappeared, to be replaced by the image of a dog that Tsali had loved as a boy. The dog stood about knee high, with a shaggy gray coat. With its penetrating eyes, it looked like a small wolf, but it had always been protective of Tsali. But in his dream, the dog's teeth were covered in blood and it growled and yipped savagely as though it were torn between attacking or retreating. Finally, in the dream, there was a wind and the steady cold rain of autumn.

That was the moment when Tsali knew what he must do. He rose slowly and felt a slight breeze from the west ruffle his gray hair—not unlike the hair on the dog in his dream. When he had gathered his blanket and axe, he started down the mountain, along the trail through the tangle of laurel that hid his camp. The axe would go with him to the end. His father's axe. The axe that Chutequutlutlih had carried that day with the soldiers because only his arms were long enough to hide it in his sleeve when they were captured. After the fight, Chutequutlutlih had wanted the gun of a soldier, so Tsali, himself, removed the axe from the face of the dead man and took it with him. He would have to give it up one more time.

As he made his way down the mountain, the ground smelled of wet leaves and within the thicket the air was still. The only sound was of the stream as it followed him down the mountain. He did not hurry. Euchella would be waiting. He could wait some more. Time was not the same thing to the Cherokees as it was to these White men. Euchella would understand.

As he stepped over the branches and weaved his way through the thicket, he remembered the dream again. The soldier had puzzled him at first, but Euchella's reference to Col. Foster made Tsali remember. The soldier in the dream must have been Foster or, more likely, the one who had come earlier, named Wool. Tsali had only heard of him. He was said not to be a bad man, one who had come to the Cherokee Nation to do a thing with which he disagreed. They said that the roundup troubled him, and that he warned his soldiers not to be brutal to the Cherokees. Yes, Tsali could see that now. That explained the tears.

The dog he understood now, too. A dog could be chased and it would run away. That was its nature. It could be chased some more and rocked and it would continue to run. It would avoid a fight. But if the dog were run until it tired, until all the ground that it could give in its territory had been taken, it would turn and attack. The attack would be furious and unexpected. The pursuer would be mauled because the sudden turn of demeanor in the dog would come without warning—like the moment he had nodded to Chutequutlutlih when his family was being hurried down the river. The axe. The soldier. The shooting. The problem was, the dog could never be trusted again. Like Spear-Finger. Yes, Tsali understood it all now, he even understood why his people called him Spear-Finger.

He looked up above the trail to where a crow was perched in a chestnut tree. As he passed the tree, the crow was silent, and Tsali gave silent thanks to the crow for the wisdom to understand the dream.

When he came to the camp of Euchella, Tsali announced his approach from a distance, implying peaceful intent. Then as he drew near, he recognized the other five Cherokees of the Oconaluftee who were with him, and the White man, Jonas Jenkins, who had lived among the Indians on Soco Creek for almost 20 years. They rose as a group and watched his approach, reading his face for signs of resistance. In a gesture that he knew to be that of the White man, Tsali took his axe—still stained from blood—from his belt and handed it to Euchella. Euchella understood that this was Tsali's attempt to handle the matter by the White man's rules, but respectfully handed back the axe.

"I will go with you," Tsali said, "but there is one

thing that you must know from me. You think that by doing this thing that you can return to the lives that you once had. You think when the soldiers leave that you will go back to your farms and fields along the river and that things will be as they were, before the soldiers came. You think that you will be Cherokee again." He paused to collect his thoughts, then went on. "The last of the Cherokee Nation was that rock where I have slept for these many nights. That was the last place where the White man could not go. Now, it is no more. The Cherokee Nation is gone. We used to have land from the big river in the north all the way to the Creek land in the south. But it is gone. The Cherokee Nation is not even those people who are moving to the place in the west. They talk about how it will be again as it was, but it is gone forever. That is what you will find when you return to your homes. There is no Cherokee Nation anymore. I had a dream and it told it."

The party of Euchella looked on impassively as he spoke. Perhaps they thought he was just a rambling old man. Perhaps he was. But the wind and the rain of his dream told him that the essence of his people would be washed and blown away and they would disappear from this land that they had once farmed and hunted and tended. The Oconaluftee Band might survive, but there would never again be a Cherokee Nation, not a nation.

The party began their trek down the valley, and the little stream became a small river and roared with the water that had been sent it by the long November rain. They passed rocks that were bigger than cabins, and pools that were dark with tinted water. As it gained energy, it roared over falls in a white froth. For several miles, they made their way past spruce trees with trunks so thick that it would have taken three or four men to reach around them. As Tsali slid past them, he ran his fingers over the bark, as he might have caressed his wife. Beyond, where hillsides gradually flattened and became fields, the little river calmed, but flowed on determinedly. In single file, the men climbed over chunks of gray granite in the stream. In contrast, here and there, round, white stones of flint shimmered through the stained water. The other men walked apart from Tsali. The curse of Spear-Finger was on him and they kept their distance as though they feared contamination.

It took them until late afternoon to reach the place where Deep Creek flowed into the wider Tuckasegee. In another two hours, the sun would set and darkness would come quickly. Out in the river, a cluster of rocks broke the rush of the stream. To a man, everyone in the party had swam there and played where the warm river current and the cold creek current mixed. Without a word, they paused for a moment to remember those times and to rest. It had been a long walk. Then, the group rose and made its way west, past an island that was half flooded beyond the bank of the swollen river. A mile away, smoke drifted from a cluster of cabins at the place called Big Bear Campground. It hung still in the air over the river and marsh beyond the cabins. Out of the doorway of the first cabin, the dark eyes of a child stared. This one would remain, this is what is left, Tsali thought to himself.

Walking past the cabins, the party grew as people joined them. They threaded their way along a path through the marsh that was created by springs that trickled out of a hillside source that was known as Big Bear Springs. For generations past memory, the Cherokees had come to this place to drink the water that ran out of the mountain. It was a mystical place, and the water had the pure taste of the porous granite that was hidden deep within the mountain. It ran cold no matter what time of year it was. Euchella stepped down to a circle of white rocks in the spring and filled a gourd and handed it to Tsali. "For your journey."

Tsali accepted the gourd and drank. Then they took him and placed him at the base of a walnut tree that stood beside a little stream where the springs collected, then stepped back. "The White man Foster said that we should ask you if you have anything to say."

Tsali felt no fear. The dream had helped him understand himself and what he had done. Not only would he soon be dead, but the rest of them would, in a way, be dead, too, and he wanted no part of that. A Cherokee Nation that was just another part of the White man's way—he wanted no part of that either. His own father would not have recognized it; his grandfather could not have conceived of it. The wind was blowing. It was his time to go. He accepted it. "Take care of my grandson."

The White man, Jenkins, stepped forward to place a blindfold over him, but Tsali waved him away. The last thing he imagined before six muskets fired simultaneously was a vision of his frail wife riding west, in the back of a wagon.

Epilogue

In the years immediately following his death, the story of Tsali's small insurrection remained quiet. But it would not remain that way because it came to serve a larger purpose.

Will Thomas continued to acquire land in his own name for what would eventually become a reservation for the Eastern Band of the Cherokees. Thomas, although White, was recognized as chief of the band, numbering just over a thousand members that were scattered throughout Western North Carolina. Euchella remained in the Qualla area, himself rising to status of a chief.

The major news of the Cherokees continued to be made by those who went west. In 1839, Major Ridge, John Ridge, and Elias Boudinot were assassinated by parties thought to be loyal to John Ross. Ross, whose wife Quatie was one of the four thousand who died during the emigration, remarried and continued as Principal Chief of the tribe until his death after the Civil War.

Chief Junaluska found his way back east, returning on foot from Oklahoma to the Snowbird Mountains where he had spent the majority of his life. He was honored by the North Carolina Legislature with a tract of 337 acres and made a citizen of the state. He died and was buried near Robbinsville, NC.

After relinquishing a second farm to the reservation, Jonas Jenkins left the Qualla area and settled not far from the Snowbirds, with his second wife. He died at the age of 67.

Col. William Foster served in the army for another year, but contracted yellow fever in Louisiana and died in 1839. He was fifty years old. His regiment memorialized him.

Lieutenant Andrew Jackson Smith, the soldier who Tsali's party had tried to kill, went on to become a general officer in the Union Army, in the War Between the States.

In spite of his acrimonious relationship with his previous commander-in-chief, Brevet General John Wool was appointed full brigadier in 1839. He distinguished himself in the Mexican War, serving under General Winfield Scott.

Andrew Jackson died in 1845, at his home in The Hermitage. One could wonder if his last mortal thoughts were of the land denied him by the Cherokees and if his revenge on them was sufficient repayment.

But what of Tsali? How did his reputation recover from being Spear-Finger to becoming the sacrificial savior of the Eastern Band of the Cherokees?

Some years after the removal, a young linguistics researcher from the Smithsonian Institute, by the name of James Mooney, made a protracted visit to the Qualla region, investigating the lore and language of the tribe. A principal resource for his study was Will Thomas. To understand the transformation of Tsali's reputation, one needs to understand Thomas' purpose at the time, and that purpose was to create a perception of responsibility for the Eastern Cherokees in the minds of White settlers and the North Carolina Legislature, a body in which he served. What better way to do this than to revise the memory of Tsali, from villain to sacrificial savior?

Mooney began publishing his findings, describing how the soldiers prodded Tsali's wife with bayonets, to make her walk faster during the trek to the stockade. There are two reasons why this account is probably untrue. First, given Will Thomas' sympathy for the Cherokees (he was the adopted son of Drowning Bear), he would not have stood by while such abuse took place. Second, based on Lieutenant Smith's careful recounting—recreation?—of the events of the revolt, he appears to be an officer who would not knowingly disobey the orders of his commanding officer, Winfield Scott. Scott had given strict orders that the Cherokees be treated humanely.

Finally, one of the Mooney reports places the choice for continued eviction of the remaining Cherokees, after the revolt, in Tsali's hands. The story implies that if Tsali chose to surrender himself to execution, then the remainder of the tribe would be allowed to stay in the East.

Facts do not support this account. Correspondence between Col. Foster and General Scott shows that those captives under Foster's control at the time of the execution were the last that were going to be rounded up and transported. The army was done with removal. Foster planned to leave with all the remaining troops even before Tsali was executed. Removal had become far more expensive than the War Department had estimated.

Perhaps, legends and heroes are created because they are needed to support the psyche of the time. Such can be said of Tsali, a common man, angry at being dispossessed and at the treatment of his family. In a moment of rage, he transformed himself into a villain. But history—and perhaps the conscience of other players in this story—needed something more of him.

ISBN 141201560-X

9 781412 015608